For My Son Steve~

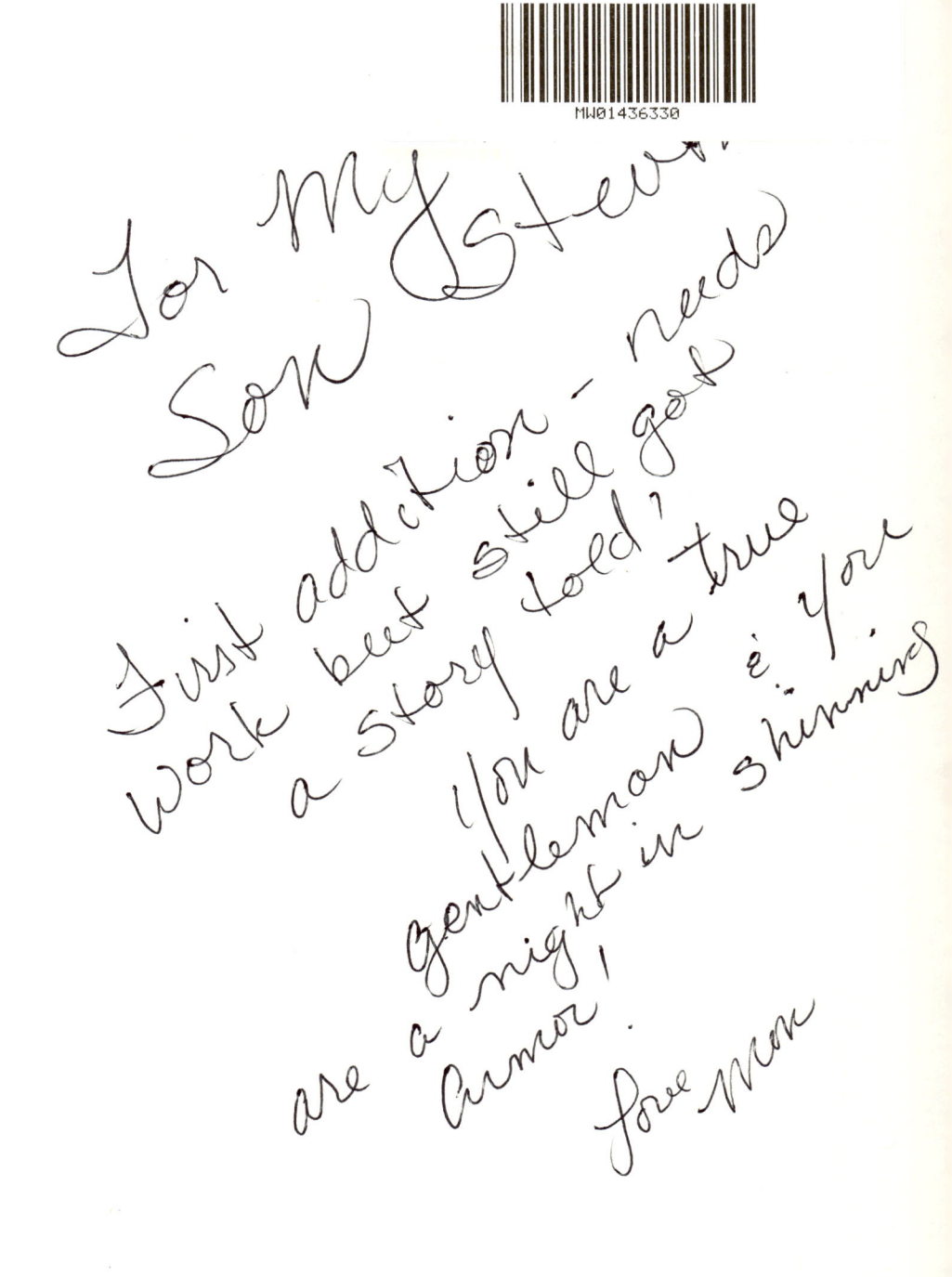

First addiction - needs work but still got a story told! You are a true gentleman & You are a night in shinning Armor!
love Mom

Little Marie Grows Up

A Fairytale In The Making

LM Phillips

Copyright © 2020 LM Phillips.

All rights reserved. No part of this book may be used or reproduced by any means, graphic, electronic, or mechanical, including photocopying, recording, taping or by any information storage retrieval system without the written permission of the author except in the case of brief quotations embodied in critical articles and reviews.

This is a work of fiction. All of the characters, names, incidents, organizations, and dialogue in this novel are either the products of the author's imagination or are used fictitiously.

All Scripture quotations are taken from The Holy Bible, New International Version®, NIV® Copyright © 1973, 1978, 1984, 2011 by Biblica, Inc.® Used by permission. All rights reserved worldwide.

Next Book: Christy On Healing Wings

LifeRich Publishing is a registered trademark of The Reader's Digest Association, Inc.

LifeRich Publishing books may be ordered through booksellers or by contacting:

LifeRich Publishing
1663 Liberty Drive
Bloomington, IN 47403
www.liferichpublishing.com
844-686-9607

Because of the dynamic nature of the Internet, any web addresses or links contained in this book may have changed since publication and may no longer be valid. The views expressed in this work are solely those of the author and do not necessarily reflect the views of the publisher, and the publisher hereby disclaims any responsibility for them.

Any people depicted in stock imagery provided by Getty Images are models, and such images are being used for illustrative purposes only. Certain stock imagery © Getty Images.

ISBN: 978-1-4897-3026-8 (sc)
ISBN: 978-1-4897-3038-1 (e)

Library of Congress Control Number: 2020915912

Print information available on the last page.

LifeRich Publishing rev. date: 08/19/2020

What readers say about this book:

CG- "Love, Love this manuscript. It's an amazing story. You know it's a great story if you keep thinking about it when you are finished reading it."

LL- "You have become a story teller. Enjoyed this very much."

I dedicate this book to all people
that have been mistreated and abused.
You are loved and not forgotten.
There is hope.

To my daughter, Melanie that continues
to encourage me to be a better me.

To my friends and family that encouraged
and gave me hope to finish this needed to be told story.
Sharon and Tana, you were the first.
Caylee you helped beyond words!

And to my loving husband, Curt,
that had faith in me to finish this book while
always giving me the support, I needed to get it written.
I am so blessed to have been rescued by him 39 years ago.
He is still my Knight in Shining Armor!

A Time to Remember

Once upon a memory. A threating midnight message would prove to be a time for me to remember why am I where I am in life? And why I am the person I have become?

My name is Marie and I am in my thirties, facing old and new challenges alike. At this point they are bringing up old memories needing to be remembered. A time which seems so far away yet does not want to be forgotten. It was full of battles that were fought and won. Now there is a new one. I am living and working in a community that its primary existence is to help rehabilitate, people that have been rescued in one way or another, from abusive situations, that range from domestic abusive environments to the deplorable sex slavery and human trafficking trade. This has had many challenges but very rewarding also. I have been driving myself so hard these past ten years, that I did not realize how my past was still haunting me. Last night brought it to the fore front again! With the past mysterious calls, so long ago were very vague and not as direct as this message became. The recorded voice used the name I was called when I was very young. He was threatening and very personal.

His low menacing voice whispered, "Hello, Little Marie. This message is for you and you alone. I want you to think long and hard about my question? Was your fiancé, Sam's death, really an accident? Timing is everything, you know! Now I will let you in on my little secrete. He is just the first of many, let's just say, to have untimely accidents. Everyone you love will die very soon. But you, Little Marie, will be the last to go. I want to watch you go through the pain of losing your loved ones, one by one. Then you can wonder when your painful accident will occur! Maybe you will want to die by then, but you will have to pay for what you have stolen from me!" Then he ended the message, with an evil laugh, proceeding the click.

After listening to the call once more, I was terrified! Who to contact, now? I needed to let everyone know that might be in danger. Mom and Dad were first of course. Then Christy, my sweet sister. With their help, we had the FBI sending out a new agent to look into the voicemail. I was hoping, they would send other agents to protect the entire family. This is the first threat in years. That must mean something. And with the man calling me "Little Marie", it became clear because of a time, I had long forgotten, Sam's untimely death was really murder. "Why? Oh no, why Lord?" I softly cried out in my lonely office. Just as I finished my plea, I felt in my spirit this loving true statement, "Pain and fear, has brought a season of running away for your own story, which will bring peace again if remembered."

I had to agree! "Yes, I have to admit though maybe not physically, I have been running away emotionally from my past. A new question now must be answered, Why I am I running?" thinking deeper still. I am beginning to realize I have been numb for years, not wanting to feel the pain that truth might bring. Deep down I have had the fear Sam died because of me and this mission that my life has been on ever since I can remember. Now the message confirms my worst fears to be true. It also confirms that the sex trafficker, known only by the name of "The Boss Man", had not been apprehended and is still on the FBI's, Most Wanted list. He has been hunting me ever since I stopped his evil plan some 20 plus years ago. Back when I was Little Marie.

Now with the realization Sam was the first of many losses to come, brought me to my knees. I found myself becoming fearful and discouraged. All I can think of at this moment, is Sam was an innocent by-stander, that fell in love with the wrong girl! Oh no, what a thing to happen. So many innocent people are hurt in this life! Why God! Please don't let it be true, but yes, I must face this now. No more running. It must be time to remember. Memories of those long-ago events may help me to understand, if ever I can, why these things had to happen. Even after all this time I still have a hard time understanding why such evil exists. It's sort of funny, with always dealing with the consequences of human trafficking, I am surprised myself I still try to think the best of people. My life's work has been about the world-wide crisis of human mistreatment, kidnapping and selling children, young woman or whatever the human slave market demands. Just recently, I heard a report that instead of winning the war against slavery, the world has more slaves now than ever before in history. Yes, the world population is so much larger than ever before, but that it still exists at all, in our so called modern "civilized" world, is very disheartening. I have become mistrustful of mankind, but I'm wired to be caring, positive and loving, so I am always hopeful when dealing with individuals. Well now that my head is spinning, I obviously need to gather my thoughts and be reminded of, why I do what I do, despite the odds. I calmed myself remembering the agents were on their way and we were protected by all kinds of security here at Healing Wings, the sanctuary my parents created when the need arrived that stormy day, so long ago. The first being we were on our own private island that was not known to the general public. Second the security was backed by top notch technology to monitor the movements of any unauthorized vessel or aircraft that approaches, is escorted away by the Coast Guard.

Now pacing in my office, I decided to make a hot cup of tea to try to relax. I realize that fear was trying to take over again! So, I stopped, stood still, closing my eyes, I whisper a little prayer. "I am so weary, and I am fighting against fear and discouragement. I want to stay hopeful, Father, but it's so hard right now! I need your help to remember why I am doing this. I guess I need to trust in You more. Please protect us from the evil one and give me the strength and wisdom to know what to do next. Among other things I need help to know how to reach through the pain and mistrust of the new girls that just arrived, especially little Beth. Thank you, Jesus. Amen."

I have always known I am not alone and that I needed to reach out in my mind and heart to open myself up to being guided by Them, The Father, Son and Spirit, instead of relying on myself to lead in my daily choses. But life seems to have a way to make me forget this until I get to the end of myself, then I remember I am not alone and turn to Them. The last few days I have been so caught up in the three new girls arriving at the community, I was not prepared for the message left on the message machine last night. Well I have lived with threats as long as I can remember and have learned about myself and the gifts I have been given, when going through those times. That is when I met Them, The Creator I Am whom I am, Father, Son and Spirit. Yes, I think time for reflection may be in order. I will go to La Bella Sirena and visit mom and dad, taking some time off to think and make a plan.

With that thought giving me encouragement, I sat down at the window looking out toward the west end of the park, remembering the day Dad and Mom showed, my sister Christy and me, this little island they purchased. They planned to build a community of healing for the rescued girls and others. That was the year when everything changed for our family and our world became a place that needed somewhere for 18 abused young girls to find their place to heal and to become part of society again. For dad, Paul, it was a chance to pull his many resources together, so with the help of some his friends, he started to develop a much-needed place, for what we all found out was a huge global problem. "Healing Wings" was established 1987 and now has grown into a thriving small town. Over the years, it has become a wonderful place that has provided the tools to heal and a chance to become the productive person, everyone is meant to be before abuse stole their dreams. The purpose always being to help people to live in society with self-worth, by using their God given gifts that were meant for a good purpose, rather than the abusive distorted lies they have come to believe about themselves from their abusive experience. We have helped hundreds of people, with most of those being girls. It is so wonderful to see the beauty that comes from ashes when someone choses to walk out the healing process. Some are so brainwashed from the abusers, that they do not want to be rescued. They will fight being helped and go back to a life of selling themselves. Freewill and freedom have to be wanted, and people of the world are still so blinded to the consequences of abuse and slavery to a human's mind and soul. There still are so many places wealthy corrupt people buy and sell young girls and boys. Trickery and kidnapping are daily occurrences even in the good old USA. This was something to bring up in the next community meeting. We might, again, be able to bring more attention to this worldwide issue. Little did I know that the next week would help do just that. Yes, discouragement seems to creep in when new girls arrive. With their

Little Marie Grows Up

hurt, afraid and mis-trusting souls, in need of rescue. One is a little girl that will only talked to me at this point. The two older girls seem to be having different reactions, to their rescue.

For right now I need to remember, beauty from ashes! Looking towards the Town Square seeing Misty Walters walking into her office. "Oh yes, remember Marie, some of the woman running the town now are from the first rescued young girls, that came to live here those many years ago. Misty has come a long way." I found myself smiling as the memories started flooding back. I was getting excited to allow myself the time to think back! Then something about a necklace I had when I was eight, popped in my head. Oh yes, the beautiful necklace, The Son gave me in my fairy world dreams, when I was Little Marie. I loved that necklace. Whatever happened to it?

Hopefully this memory is the one I needed to encourage me to go back past the night Sam died, past the pain of loss, to put an end to that evil man that admitted to the murder! Looking out at the fall colors changing on the trees in the town square, and the beauty of the town that began with the rescue of those girls long ago. Why have I forgotten about my time as a child? Well, no one really believed me about my fairy world I had experience, but it was true! Wasn't it? I am going to have to find that necklace. Then smiling, I whispered, "Thank you for the reminder Holy Spirit, my story was a kind of a Fairy tale in the making, it's the place to start. After all, I had grown up here, myself, because of what happened those many, many years ago, when I was, Little Marie. Deep in thought I was startled to hear a loud knock on the door. Putting my Tea down on the way to open the door. I ask, "May I help you?" Then hearing Jenny's nervous voice. "Oh hello, Jenny. Is something wrong?" I responded while opening the door.

"Yes, yes, the little girl we call Little Beth, has run off into the woods. We have a search party getting together and thought you and your hound would be a great help. You seem to be the only one she will respond to since she arrived." Jenny answered while following me out the front door.

"Oh, my goodness. I have been so caught up in the message I didn't visit her this morning. Come let's get Buddy and you can show me where she ran into the forest. I think I have just the thing to help Little

Beth trust me, but we need to find her first!" I grabbed my cell phone and jacket with my keys and ran out with Jenny our towns newspaper editor. We are a wonderful community and will continue to be so, if I have anything to do with it.

Buddy was so happy to go for an outing, but he got serious when I gave him a big sniff of little Beth's toy bunny she had dropped while running into the south end of the forest. This was my favorite place to walk him, so I was very optimistic we would find her. I told the search party to search around the outskirts and let Buddy and me have a bit of time to see if we could find her. I didn't want everyone scaring her more than she already was. Our new cell phone tower on the hill will help us communicate anywhere on the island and I had a plan forming, being inspired to tell the story of when Little Marie grows up!

"Come on Buddy let's find Beth." We bounded into the forest and immediately buddy picked up her scent. "Now Buddy quiet, no baying, you might scare, little Beth." I pated his head then called out "Hello, it's Miss Marie, I'm here Little Beth. Please, come out." Buddy started to tug on her leash toward the little creek to the left. We walk slowly down the path with me calling out, "I know you must be scared. I was too when I was your age when I was out in the woods alone. Buddy and I have a story we would like to tell you, but you will have to come out and sit with us to hear it. It is a story filled with beautiful Angels, Mermaids and Fairy's! With a little girl just like you. She becomes a hero." Stopping at a large fallen log with soft moss coving it, I sat down for a moment to listen. I could hear something just ahead so I waited, hoping it was her and she would come to me. Buddy sat leaning on my leg sensing he needed to be calm while looking at me then towards the forest. A minute, then another. Am I doing the right thing? As that thought crossed my mind, I saw the sweet face of little Beth peeking out through the small patch of baby fir trees growing just under the towering old cedar tree, I was sitting under. I felt I needed to let her choose to come to me, so I sat there, saying "Well Buddy you can lay down and rest. We have found little Beth." Buddy laid down at the command. "Do you want to hear the story? It is full of adventures and hero's." I said softly. That seemed to do it. The little brown-haired girl came out from hiding and walked cautiously towards me and sat down on the end of log, a distance away, still not completely trusting. I could see the curiosity, in her big round dark eyes. Curiosity was overcoming her fear.

Her soft voice rang through the late summer afternoon. "Yes please, I would like to hear the story." she said very quietly.

"I would love to tell you the story. I have not told it in a very long time. It is a very special story about a girl named Little Marie... but first I need to tell Jenny you are okay. When you ran off everyone was worried about you, sweetheart. I will tell her, Buddy and I found you, so they do not worry anymore." I texted Jenny to let the search party know that everything was fine, that I had found her and gave our location, but to let me handle things. I would text later.

While she sat watching me, she asked "Why would anyone worry about me?" Looking at her expression on her face, I saw she was completely surprised we cared! All I could do was smiled and say, "Well we do care about you Little Beth and I hope, one day you will understand how much."

Then I started the story of my life, I had never really told before, well not like this.

Loss of Innocence

ONCE UPON A TIME, *in a place like many other places, there was a small family with a Mommy, a Daddy and two young daughters. This tale is not starting with a very happy ever after moment for Mommy. Daddy was not to be her "Prince in shining armor." Her children were the only blessings that came from that union. Mommy, Christy, and Little Marie all had to move on, to an apartment.*

Little Marie was 8 years old and did not understand why they moved from the big house and why her Daddy was not living with them. What she did understand was that things had changed, and she didn't like i! Mommy was always dropping them off at babysitters or school. Why did she have to work somewhere in town and Little Marie could not get to go with her, instead of the babysitters? This was hard on Little Marie because Mommy never had worked at a real job before. She was always the one home taking care of everything, but that changed and Little Marie missed her Mommy.

Christy at 13 was tall like her daddy. She was a bit shy and completely kindhearted. She was handling this upsetting change by doing what she was told to do, being quiet and helpful. She knew Daddy and Mommy had not been happy for many years, no matter what she did they always quarreled. After the divorce had happened, Mommy needed help with Little Marie and everything else. Daddy being gone was very hard on her because she loved him deeply. One thing that helped both the girls, was Mommy didn't cry as much now. So Christy was trying to be a good girl and not be a problem.

Mommy promised them this was to be a good change for the three of them and they will understand in time. Yet Little Marie didn't understand at all! She could only think of herself and all that she missed. Mommy at

Little Marie Grows Up

home, Daddy, her big house, her yard where she could have had a puppy. But now, she did not have any of those things in an Apartment! During this time in her life she would wake up counting her disappointments, instead of her blessing, getting herself so worked up, first thing in the morning, that she complained and cried the rest of the day. That was not like her natural sweet nature' but she was missing all the things she loved about her eight-year-old life. She usually was a happy girl, looking for animals and nature everywhere she went. Christy tried to entertain her, but Little Marie was much more stubborn and could not always be consoled by her sister.

Everyone was tired and stressed but over the next few weeks, things started to improve for all of them. The girls had new friends at school. And life seemed to move forward.

One day Mommy had come home with a new dress that made her blue eyes sparkle. Little Marie was so impressed with how pretty her mommy looked, she was smiling ear to ear. Mommy told the girls that she had a special date with a really nice man tonight and the neighbor lady would be by at 6:00pm to babysit. She looked at Little Marie and saw her smile fall a bit then her little girl said, "Oh Mommy he will think you are so beautiful!" and ran up to her for a big hug. That was a nice change.

The babysitter showed up, but it was not the neighbor lady it was her husband. Mommy knew him so being sweet and naïve she said okay and told them all, she would not be late. The man seemed nice enough to the girls and so when he sat down and opened a beer in the kitchen, Little Marie went to play in her room and Christy went to the living room to read.

Once it was dark outside the man got up and one at a time, he wanted to talk to the girls alone. He took Little Marie first into Mommy's room and closed the door. After showing her, he had a gun, he did bad things to her. Touching her in her private places and making her touch him. She was in shock and didn't know what to do." I stopped speaking, now seeing Beth move closer to me, until she was sitting almost in my lap.

I, of course, left out the dirty details of what happened, for Little Beth's sake and mine. I leaned closer so her shoulder slightly leaned on my arm, being careful not to overwhelm her with touch. I began, again "Then he put her to bed with a terrible threat he would kill her mommy, if she told anyone what he did. Little Marie cried herself to sleep. Little Marie found out later, the bad man also hurt Christy her sister." I stopped for a moment as memories flooded my head and again forgiveness was needed. How could I tell her what really happened to Christy? Remembering that the "bad man", what we called him, actually blamed us! He said "This is all your fault. You girls are so lovely to look at, but I can't touch. Day after day I watch in secret. This was too good of an opportunity, that fell in my lap, with my wife getting sick and all. I just couldn't help myself!" You and your sister better keep your mouths shut and never tell anyone or I will kill you, your sister and your Mommy. You hear me.!" He pointed the gun in her face one more time before closing the door and went to grab another beer, forgetting the phone had rang. She said she fell to the ground for a moment then told her self she must be a "good girl" and do what she was told to protect her family! That gun was so real and the thought of losing her family made her mind up for her. She was never going to tell anyone ever about this terrible night. She just couldn't! I'm so glad she finally could tell me.

But this was not for this story, to this little girl. Looking down now, at little Beth's face, I can only imagine what she has been through. She looked up at me with tears in her eyes. So, I thought to ask, "Do you want to tell me what happened to you?" She looked down and shook her head no, but whispered "What happens, next?"

"Well, when Mommy did not get an answer to her call home, she had her date take her home early. Everything seemed fine. She asked the bad man why he didn't answer the phone. He said he must have been in the restroom when the phone rang, apologized and said good night, closing the door behind him. Well that was a little strange but the girls were tucked in sleeping and she was tired from a wonderful date, so she went to bed without any idea of the unthinkable things the man had done to her children!

The next morning Christy came to sit on her sister's bed. They hugged and cried a bit, then getting serious, they agreed not to say anything to anyone. They would have to try to forget the bad man and the bad night. They both went throughout the day in a daze keeping to themselves. The third-grade teacher and aide were surprised to not have to deal with Little Marie's moodiness, she was uncommonly quiet and withdrawn, but for

Little Marie Grows Up

the teachers it was a welcome change. And Christy was very quiet but that was not uncommon for her, so no one noticed the girls pain that day.

At dinner, Mommy told the girls that her date from last night, Paul, wanted to take them **all** out on a date! "What do you think, girls?" After some prodding, Little Marie was the first to respond. "Ah, where would he take us?"

"The movies I think." Mommy said with a smile, knowing that would get them jumping for joy because they loved going to the movies and it had been a long, long time since they had all gone to see one. But instead she got a sad sounding "That will be nice" from Christy and "Do we know this man?" from Little Marie.

"His name is Paul and a very nice man, I like a lot. He would like to take us all tomorrow night." Mommy answered while she picked up the dishes. The girls looked at each other and said in unison, "OK" and walked away to get ready for bed.

"Ok. We will make plans." Mommy called out to them with a puzzled look. *What has gotten into those girls putting themselves to bed? I will find out later. I need to call Paul and except his wonderful invite.* That was all that was on her mind.

Now the next part of the story is why we call the town "Healing Wings." I stopped to see if I should continue and seeing Little Beth was listening intently, I did.

On Healing Wings

"We have them in our grasp!" Fear told Lies.
"Yes, our little plan seems to be working." Lies said
seeing the odds had turned in their favor.
"We must stay alert using all our wits, so our Master's plan will have victory."
Fear smiled while he looked around at the trembling girls in the cave.
"We have the upper hand now." Lies smirked but then remembering that truth
was always right behind trying to catch them and when it did it always won!
Fear and Lies flew away staying ahead of their enemy.

Now Little Marie had become fearful of the dark since that night, so Christy put a little night light by her bed for her. As she was falling asleep, she was thinking of the nice man mommy said was taking them to see a big movie. The girls first date. She smiled as she dozed off. Happy not to think of the other man.

Awhile later she found herself in a dream standing in a large room with books on the walls with a small window on one side. The door was closed, with her family and friends all around her. Everyone was talking and laughing until she looked into each face. One by one they faded into the darkness that was now taking over the room. When her sister was the last to fade away, the room went completely dark. She could not see anything. It was pitch black, but she knew that someone was still there.

"Where did everyone go?" she cried out.

"They all are gone. We took them. You are all alone with us!" Two wicked voices cackled from the darkness. Fear grabbed her arm and Lies whispered into her ear, "There is no one to help you."

Dropping to her knees Little Marie called out into the darkness "Oh Please Help me. I cannot do this alone! Daddy, Mommy! Someone save me?"

Little Marie Grows Up

At that very moment, a strong lovely voice filled the room. "Do not be afraid! I am here."

When Little Marie opened her eyes, she was amazed to see a beautiful Angel floating high above the floor. The light flowing from her was illuminating the room with truth that Little Marie was all right, which brought peace to her trembling heart. She looked into the Angels face, thinking to herself, "Thank you, your light is beautiful."

The angel smiled saying, "You are most welcome my sweet Little Marie. My name is Samantha. I have been sent by The I Am, The Father, The Son and Holy Spirit. They want you to know how much They love you and that you will never be alone." Samantha glided down to stand next to Little Marie, all the while looking up so Little Marie followed her gaze. It was an astonishing sight of, two small winged creatures trying to stay out of the light up in the corner of the room. They had pointy faces, with pointy noises and ears. Their wings were black and had burnt edges making them look very wicked but at the same time, harmless too.

"Oh my, how wonderful to be able to see but I don't understand? Who are they? Why did I not see them, before? They seemed much bigger in the dark!" Little Marie questioned in amazement.

"You will only be able to see them if you seek the truth with all your heart and mind, but for now my little one, you asked for help and I am here to share with you the love and protection of the Savior." She turned and shined her full light on the two small winged creatures calling out to them, "Fear and Lies! Be gone in the name of the Son who paid the price so Little ones such as this one will be free from the curse of this world forever more." At once Fear and Lies flew out the window that had opened at Samantha's words, which now slammed shut after their hasty exit.

Little Marie stood there amazed at what she saw and felt a love, peace and protection flow through her that she had never experienced. With tears of joy she asked the Angel, "What is the Sons name?"

"Jesus the Christ is the Son's name. For I Am – is the Creator of all the Universe and mankind calls Him God. He loves you." The Angel Said. "For God so loved the world that He gave His only beloved Son, to pay the price for mankind's choice of dependence on self rather than the Creator. He overcame even death itself to free mankind. If you believe in Jesus as the Son of The I Am- then the Creator becomes your Father and you can use the Son's name to cast out these filthy demons like Fear and Lies. But be aware the enemy does not want you to become what God has created you to be, so he is always trying to steal your innocence and your God given dreams and gifts. He uses his fallen angels like Fear and Lies to name a few by attacking the young and old, alike. The Enemy himself is a fallen angel and angry with mankind, so he cleverly uses pain and suffering to cause people to hurt others and themselves. Hurting people hurt people.* (Joyce Meyers) Those that do not seek the Creator and The Son only find more pain and no healing for their soul."

"Like that bad man?" Little Marie looked down at the floor, with tears in her eyes.

"Yes. You know Little Marie Jesus loves him also, but the man is lost and does not know he is loved. The man has many demons he listens too and is in a lot of pain. Jesus will help you forgive this man if you ask Him."

"What? Why would I want to do that! He hurt me and my sister!" She cried out.

"I understand my dear. Yet when you forgive those who hurt you, His Love- Jesus' love will heal all wounds. Mercy and Grace are given to those who ask for them, for all mankind falls short of the pureness of the Creator, therefore they are separated from Him because of their bad choices but Jesus paid the price for those choices, this sets them free to show forgiveness to those that hurt them, as they have been forgiven for their bad choices. You will be forgiven as you forgive others."

"Why do I need to be forgiven? I have not made bad choices? Or have I?" Marie looked up through her tear-filled lashes.

"All fall short of the glory of the pure love and goodness of the Creator... I seem to remember some selfish outbursts from a little girl when her Mommy needed her to behave and be patient. Your pain made you do that! All of mankind needs help with all those types of attitudes and ways. God wants a relationship with them to help them with that. He will send the Helper, His Holy Spirit." With that the Angel kissed her on the forehead and Little Marie, woke up instantly remembering the love, peace and freedom that came from the Angel of Jesus. She found herself saying, "Jesus I believe. Please forgive me and help me to forgive too. Thank you." Then she opened her eyes, looked around and saw it was still dark but for the little night light Christy plugged in for her. Ah Sweet Christy, she loved *her sister so much that she found herself saying a prayer for her to know Jesus, also! Feeling very happy she fell back to sleep with a changed heart.*

I look down and found Beth's eyes big and wide again, she was listening intently to a story I had never told in detail like this before. I was remembering details I had forgotten. I had not thought of starting where I started but it was the beginning, this will take some time to tell, so as the idea came in my head, I decided to take little Beth to the lake cabin down the path, instead of back to where she ran away from. I called to let Jenny know my plan and she said she would bring supply's out to the cabin, by early evening.

So, I continued, "The next morning, Little Marie woke up remembering her wonderful dream and it seemed so real. It must have been because she did trust Jesus, the Son of the Creator God, now. She also believed in Angels too. She beamed with the joy of feeling so loved. She was bouncing down the hall and almost ran into Christy.

"Watch, where you're going!" Christy mumbled while she jumped out of the way.

"Sorry sis. Love you and so does Jesus" Little Marie sang out, with a hug and a kiss, then before Christy could respond, she scooted by. What is with her? Christy thought. And walked into the kitchen.

At breakfast Mommy surprised the girls, telling them," We are going to dinner and a movie with Mr. Paul, tonight."

"Yay" Said Little Marie and Christy just smiled.

Mommy was happy to see the girls respond with more excitement then yesterday. The girls went to school looking forward to going out with Mommy and meeting Mr. Paul. It was their first date ever!

Christy thought this would help her keep her mind off you know, and Little Marie was already forgetting for some reason."

Thinking it was time for a break, I stood up and stretched, asking, "Beth would you like to go to the cabin up the path with me and we can stay there for a while? Then I can tell you the whole story if you want? We will have all the time we need."

Beth got up and looked around seeming to trust me, but not quit knowing why. After her experiences she had a very hard time trusting anyone, I am sure. She said, "I like the story so far, specially the part about Samantha the angel, being stronger than those wicked creatures,

Fear and Lies." I was surprised to hear her answering excitedly. "Yes, that would be so nice! Thank You."

The two of us, with Buddy, started the short walk to the cabin, down the path that we were already on. It was part of the private lake of Healing Wings community. It was only a short hike through the woods from the community center and my office. I felt safe there. I like how secluded the cabin is, with a cliff on one side blocking any entrance to the west with the lake in between.

This day was turning out to be very special, I thought. I smiled to myself and thanked Jesus. I was ready to remember, and I could see this might be the way to start the healing process for little Beth. We found the cabin quiet and ready for us to get comfortable for a good long story that may help this little girl. After snacking on the sandwich makings that where in the pantry and sipping on tea I made, we sat in the big leather couch by the big window that looked out on to the lake with the sun starting its slow descent in the midday sky. Summer days are longer up here in the Pacific North West but with the mountains on the west side it got dark early here, from there shadowing height.

"OK so where did I leave off?" I asked

"Little Marie was happy because she found power in the name of the Son. The Angel Samantha showed her in her dream. Her sister and her were excited about their date with Mr. Paul" Beth sat back to listen feeling safe for the first time that she can remember, she told me later.

"I am so happy you came here with me. I guess I needed to tell this story and you are the perfect one to hear it. Thank you, Little Beth for being here to listen." I hugged her as I continued;

The First Date

"Mommy, Christy and Little Marie were excited for tonight's big date with Mr. Paul, but all for different reasons.

First off, Little Marie was excited to go to the movies and watch a fantasy world come to life, with all the color, music and stories on a giant movie screen. She loved to play pretend at home because reading was still difficult for her to do by herself, she had to rely on her own imagination. Mommy and Christy read to her wonderful stories, so she used those stories and her imagination to make her life enjoyable when she found herself lonely. Now it had been a really long time since she had gone anywhere at night let alone to the movies. That made it really exciting! Little Marie wanted to wear a fancy frilly dress, but Mommy said it was not appropriate for their date as she pointed to a new outfit she had laid out on Little Marie's bed. Christy's bed had one too! Little Marie's new outfit was a pretty new top that was lavender with a white sweater and light blue caprices with white sandals that had sparkles all over. Trying them on she danced around in front of the mirror happily.

But on the other hand, Christy, was hoping with all her heart that going out with this new friend of Mommies was a good thing. She was good at pretending like Little Marie also, but she didn't do it for fun. She did it to be able to run away in her mind from the bad things in life, like Daddy being gone and that bad, bad man. She learned to not trust men now especially after that terrible night, but tried to not think about it, let alone deal with it. So, to make it all ok, she could pretend it didn't happen and go on being the good girl Mommy needed her to be. She was excited to wear the new outfit Mommy had bought. She needed to find a way to forget, she had to believe she could. Her new top on her bed was a deep turquoise blue with a white sweater and white long slim jeans with cute turquoise sparkly sandals. She loved her knew outfit, too.

Mommy was happy to give her girls new outfits to finally meet Paul. "What do you think my darling's? It's your favorite colors." she said with a smile. The girls ran up and gave her a hug with a giggle.

The sisters danced around their room with laughter and joy. They seemed to like their pretty new clothes which touched Mommy's heart deeply." What a memory I thought, and when Mom shared with me years after her and Paul were married, the hopes she had at that time, I sat for a moment to remember what she had said. I could add on.

"Mommy was hoping this was the start of a wonderful life! She knew she needed to take it slow with Paul. He seemed so genuine, but they had only gone out a couple of times, before tonight." She had to make sure he was right for them all! After some of the smooth talkers she had met before now she was not so naive.

Mommy looked lovely. She turned around in front of the mirror one last time with a smile, then went to get the girls going. They all jumped at the sound of the doorbell. In the hallway she was greeted by her two excited beautiful girls.

At the same time, they said, "Thank you Mommy, we love our new clothes!" She smiled, then told them to wait in the living room while she answered the door.

It was Paul on time, with flowers for Mommy and a single pink rose for each of the girls. He waited in the living room with the shy girls, while she found a vase in the kitchen for her beautiful big bouquet of flowers. She came back into the room seeing the girls leaning forward completely enthralled in something Paul was quietly telling them. When they all saw her come into the room, the girls jumped back and smiled. Paul smiled too and walked over to Mommy, taking her hand in his and then raising it to his lips to kiss it, he complimented her by saying, "You look lovely tonight, my dear". She blushed and the girls giggled. "Shall we go?" he said as he led her to the door. "I hope you girls like movies filled with Adventure and Fantasy?" He winked.

Little Marie was the first to chime in. "Oh yes we do." She spoke for all of them! "I hope it's a "Happy ever after" movie..." her voice trailed off thinking about her own story was getting better

Little Marie Grows Up

Christy just looked away. It was not quiet going that way for her, yet!

"Paul this is so wonderful of you to take us all out tonight." Mommy hung onto his arm as they walked toward a shiny red sports car. "Is this your car?" they all said in unison.

Paul, smiling again, instead of answering he just walked over to the sports car and opened the door for all of them. He pushed the seat back forward for the girls to get in the small backseat. He then helped Mommy into the front seat.

"We cannot take too long at the restaurant because the movie starts at 8 o'clock sharp" Paul said.

They left for the movie theater tummies full, with just enough time to get there. It was dark outside, so the lights and the sounds were so exciting. When they arrived Little Marie and Christy looked around trying to see everything. All the different people going out with their families. What a wonderful time. They found seats together towards the middle of the theater to watch a beautifully animated story with Mermaid adventures, with love conquering in the end. The adults enjoyed it more than they expected. They were all very happy on the drive home.

Little Marie was still completely enthralled with the movie on the way home as she fell asleep dreaming of Mermaids and adventures...

Paul helped Mommy tuck the girls into bed."

Little did they know this was the beginning to a wondrous adventure for them all.

Jeremiah 29:11 (NIV)
[11] For I know the plans I have for you," declares the L ORD*, plans to prosper you and not to harm you, plans to give you hope and a future*

Mermaid & Fairy Dreams

It was such a magical night out with Mr. Paul and her family. Little Marie was tucked in her bed with a smile on her fac. After falling fast asleep, she started having a wonderful dream. She was a fairy with beautiful wings. She was flying back and forth over the edge of the rocks on a beach and was compelled to look out to sea for something. Listening very intently, she could barely hear a voice calling to her. The sound of the waves hitting the rocks made it hard to hear or understand. There it was again but a touch louder.

"Where are you ...." a small shrill voice came closer, then all of a sudden, a simmering yellow haired Mermaid was sitting on the rock beside her. The Mermaid was the size of a dolphin with a long glistening aqua blue tail hanging over the rock, still dipping into the ocean. Her body was that of a young beautiful woman with her long blond wet curls hanging down to her waist. She was adorned with all kinds of shinny shells on her neck, wrists and in her hair. When she smiled you could see her teeth were very sharp unlike a human's and she spoke in a quiet, high pitched voice.

"My name is Crystal."

"Are you the one calling out to me?" Little Marie asked.

"Well yes and no!" Crystal, the Mermaid Queen of the Pacific Ocean, responded, "I have been looking for my lost sister Sarah, for a long, long, time now. So, I was calling out to her but I also need all the help I can get to find her so I am very happy you are here to hear my call, dear little fairy."

"What? Fairy, oh my yes." Little Marie giggle as she spun around. "I'm a fairy how can that be? It is very nice though and I would love to help if I can?" Little Marie said with a smile of amazement. "What is your sister's name? Is she a mermaid too?" She found herself asking.

Little Marie Grows Up

"Sarah. Yes, she is like me but..." She said while pointing to the land and the forest. "I fear she has gone into the forest and will never come back! She will become human."

"How could she do that if she is a mermaid like you?" Little Marie asked pointing to the Mermaids tail. "How can she be on land?"

"Watch this. I will show you." Crystal lifted her tail out of the water and like magic she had legs. She stood up and swirled around. Right before Little Marie eyes, a pretty blue dress formed around Crystals little body as she spun on legs that replaced her tail.

"That's amazing. How did you do that?" Little Marie asked yet another question.

Not being bothered by all the questions Crystal just answered "You will find Little Marie; Mermaid Queens have many powers. Only the children of the King can do this wonderful thing, giving us a choice to live in the ocean or land. We can never be too far from water though!" She said.

"Why not?" Little Marie asked.

"Because if we are away from a body of water to long, we lose are ability to change back. We can never go back to being a Mermaid." With another tear rolling down her check she continued, "That is why I am so concerned because the time is counting down, by the day and I may never find her in time."

Finished saying that, the pretty mermaid queen, took off running down the beach toward the forest, with Little Marie flying after her.

"Oh, I have forgotten how nice it is to feel the sand beneath my toes!" Crystal ran up to the edge of the forest a little out of breath and looking back, glad to see Little Marie right behind her.

"I know I ask a lot of questions," Little Marie said, looking down for a moment. "I am very curious I guess, and I would like to help. Please tell me the story of Sarah your sister?"

Crystal started pacing back in forth in front of a path that led into the dark forest.

"She ran away." She finally answered

Little Marie sat down on a large piece of drift wood to listen and try not to interrupt.

So, Crystal started the tale, "Many years ago, when we were younger, my parents, the King and Queen of all the Waters, had to decide which daughter would be the next queen of the Pacific. We have one King and his wife Queen over all the waters on the earth but the princesses, the royal daughters, are chosen to rule over the many different seas, oceans, rivers and lakes. The daughters of the King are who become these Queens. When a new Queen was needed for the Pacific Ocean, the King needed to choose who is it would be. Sarah and I where next in line, being the two oldest. Now please understand, this is an honor and a privilege of being the daughter of the King. It is also a big responsibility to a new life protecting and ruling the waters that Our Father chooses for us. Sarah understood this as I do but she had already hoped and longed to be the Atlantic Ocean Queen because she had fallen in love with a man that lived on a beautiful ship that sailed back and forth across it." Crystal stopped pacing and sat beside Little Marie on the log. Looking Little Marie straight in her eyes she explained... "Oh, when our father found out about this love affair, he all but exploded. He did not approve, to say the least. He thought by choosing her to live in the Pacific as the Queen he would alleviate two problems he was facing at the same time. Getting her away from that human and filling the open spot for the Pacific Ocean Queen. Before we knew it, he gathered all the family and officials together to announce that Sarah was the next chosen Queen of the Pacific. Sarah was so upset. She had no idea and was caught off guard. With this being a public announcement, she had to accept, but later that night she made a snap decision. At the very next opportunity she had, she would run far away to an unknown place. She left that very night, leaving a note for me explaining everything. We have not seen her since." Crystal looked into the forest again.

Little Marie was so moved by the story that she flew up the path a ways ahead, before looking back and asking, "Why are you looking here?"

"I believe she must be somewhere on the land because father cannot find her in all the waters on earth. She was not even with the sailor she loved. He appointed me the Pacific Ocean Queen and then went out in search of her." Crystal finished saying with a faraway look in her eyes.

"Oh my, that should not be. How can I help?" Little Marie asked, while flying back to be beside Crystal again.

Little Marie Grows Up

"Well you might be just the one to help." Crystal looked around then leaned closer to Little Marie. "Where did you come from?"

"Ah" Little Marie looked around thinking for a moment then she replied, "I think the Creator, I AM sent me?"

Crystals eyes widened and she announced, "Oh then you must be the one to help!"

Crystal then jumped up and ran down the path to a large old growth tree and waved into the dark woods. Little Marie followed her but didn't see who she was waving at.

A light summer breeze began to blow their hair back and Crystal giggled. "I have not seen Amber Wind in a while." Just then out of the forest popped a beautiful dark hair Fairy. The breeze stopped.

Startled Little Marie stumble back forgetting she could fly. "Where did you come from?"

"Everywhere! Her name is Amber Wind, Amber meet Little Marie." Crystal chimed in with a big smile before Amber had time to respond.

Amber seemed to float rather than fly over to where Little Marie had landed in front of the tall old growth tree. Bowing then, looking right into Little Marie's eyes, she said, "We have been waiting for you!"

Before Little Marie could speak Amber floated back to Crystal saying, "We are close to locating them." Then the breeze turned into a cold brisk wind as Amber beckoned the two to enter the forest. Shivering from the sudden change in temperature Little Marie and Crystal followed Amber Wind into the tall trees. The wind stopped instantly as they moved past a pair of large trees on either side of the path that led even deeper into the darkness of the forest.

Amber Wind stopped and spoke to Crystal first, "Now that you have found her and brought her here, you can return to the sea to find your father and tell him the good news that help is here."

Crystal curtsied to both Amber and Little Marie, saying "Thank I AM the Creator!" She kissed Little Marie's hand and ran back down the path to the Ocean, looking back only once, with a wink and a smile. She then dove into the water just as a wave hit the rocks, popping up long enough to wave a "good bye for now" to the two fairies she knew were looking through the trees.

Before Little Marie could ask another question, Amber grabbed her arm and in a loud voice said, "Hurry, follow me!"

Surprised by all that was happening around her Little Marie didn't move let alone follow Amber right away. She thought–Maybe she should find out from someone else to see if she should follow this Amber Fairy."

Amber turned around as if she read Little Marie's mind and stopped and let go of Little Marie's arm. She just hovered in place waiting for something. As Little Marie looked around, she was surprised to see another beautiful Fairy standing right next to her.

"Don't be afraid Little Marie, I am your Fairy God Mother or Guardian Angel if you prefer." As Little Marie looked into the eyes of her FGM she was filled with love and peace. She felt a connection to this Golden-haired fairy. All her doubt and fear had gone once Christina was there.

"The great I AM the Creator of All the universe has chosen me to help you on the adventures in your life. I'm so glad you have come here where we can meet, I have watched over you since you were born. Do remember me?" Christina asked. Little Marie just shook her head No, while smiling from ear to ear.

"Well, now I can show you things that will help you have victory in your life. You have taken the first step into the life you were created to have, as each of I AM's creations who are given the choice. But now we must hurry and follow Amber Wind for she has an important mission I AM the Son has for us." As she spoke of the Son, the large clear sparkling stone held at the top of a long wooden staff with three braided bands of gold, started to glow brightly, lighting a path that led into the dark dense forest. They started to move forward when Little Marie spoke up, "The Son of The I AM- Jesus? Is that who you are talking about?"

"Yes, my sweet, Jesus the Son & the I AM!" Christina answered.

With that answer Little Marie flew with them both, into the deep dark of the old growth forest with only the light of the crystal in Christina's staff to guide them. She could hear a lovely song being played and sung by the forest, while they flew.

Little Beth seemed to be hanging on every word, so I continued.

Into The Woods We Go

Psalm 23
[1] *The* L<small>ORD</small> *is my shepherd, I lack nothing.*
[2] *He makes me lie down in green pastures,*
he leads me beside quiet waters,
[3] *he refreshes my soul.*
He guides me along the right paths
for his name's sake.
[4] *Even though I walk*
through the darkest valley, [a]
I will fear no evil,
for you are with me;
your rod and your staff,
they comfort me.

In the deep of the forest there was a joyous noise. A gathering of fairies from far and near were coming together in the small clearing near the northeast corner of the forest. They were preparing for something or someone. In the center of the clearing there was a table shaped like a large horseshoe around a fire pit with all shapes and sizes of pots and pans, boiling and bubbling with all kinds of foods and colorful liquids. Some of the fairies were busy cooking, with a few setting the white and green linens and dishes around the table, while others were decorating the table with flowers and fairy dust. The blue and white toad stools were placed for seating on both sides of the horseshoe table. A lovely cake was placed on a small table by the center of the horseshoe. There were also various creatures helping with all that needed to be done. Everyone there hummed and buzzed while they worked.

Little Marie started to hear another musical sound coming from the direction they were headed. It was also getting a little brighter as they came closer to the beautiful melody.

Amber flew ahead a bit, then turned around hovering with more excitement, then she had shown before, "We are almost there. They are all singing. Do you hear them Little Marie?" she asked.

"Yes, I do Amber it is so very lovely, I was going to ask who is playing those instruments?" Little Marie replied.

"You will see!" With a laugh she flew ahead again. A perfect breeze started to blow and the tall Aspen trees that lined the edge of the forest started to sway with their beautiful white trunks and little heart shaped leaves flickering seeming to say "Welcome, please come to the meadow!" The sweet aroma of food cooking on the camp fire was carried on that breeze to Little Marie causing her to realize she was hungry. Looking through the trees she saw the most wonderous sight she had seen yet, a beautiful Fairy party.

"We are almost to the gathering place. There we will get some much-needed food and rest." Christina pointed ahead. They flew through the trees into the open meadow that was called the Gathering Place and stopped right in front of a large rosy checked creature, made up partially of flesh and blood, but clay and bark also. "This is Nanny, our wonderful mother of the forest." The strange but sweet looking creature turned around from telling everyone to hurry up and jumped back when she saw who it was standing there. She jumped again this time it was for joy, causing a little moss to go flying into the air. "Oh, it's so wonderful to see you Queen Christina. Oh, beautiful Amber Wind thank you for the lovely breeze my dear!" Then turning to Little Marie, she curtsied and held out her hand saying, "You must be Little Marie. We are so pleased you could come to our little gathering. Please come and sit down." As Nanny started to lead Little Marie to the table, everyone stopped what they were doing and looked around to see who had just arrived. All at once the fairies rushed over to welcome their new guests. They were so excited that they had forgotten their manners and flitted about Little Marie like little puppies fighting over a treat. Fairy dust was flying everywhere.

Christina had to intervene and shoed them away! "Now is this the way you treat our guest of honor? Please calm down and we can introduce all of you to her one at a time." Christina led Little Marie to have the seat of honor at the middle of the horse shoe table, next to the cake. Little Marie was amazed to hear that she was the guest of honor! "What? Who me? What do you mean, Guest of Honor? How did you know I was coming here?" She cried out, through all the commotion.

"We will have time to talk about all that later, these fairies have been waiting to meet you." Christina said as she looked around at the very beautiful but also very different fairies that had attended the party, now lining up to meet Little Marie.

One at a time the little fairies and the forest creatures stood patiently in line to meet Little Marie. She was so excited to meet them all. Fairies like Kim Song Joy of the flowers, Alana the Island Fairy and Mercy an Ocean Fairy to name a few. They were all beautiful and unique in their own ways.

Little Marie sat back in wonder, after the last woodland creature from the line walked away.

This was something she knew she would never forget! Even if it was a dream. The smaller fairies flew over the table setting down plates and bowls of different looking foods. An elf like creature filed the glasses with a sparkling liquid. The food and drink smelled so good and looked as delicious, so for the first time she could remember picky Little Marie didn't care what she was eating or drinking. Eating everything to her hearts content. This was truly a feast and she sat for a moment to take in the amazing surroundings, she found herself enjoying. All the beautiful fairies were eating, talking and serving each other. Amber Wind sat on her left and Christina sat at her right, who was quietly talking to Miracle, the fairy of hope that was next to her.

Nanny announced it was time to cut the cake and start the next part of the celebration! "Night will be here soon and there is still much to do!" Several fairies flew off to cut the cake then those in the band gathered to make their music. Little Marie was surprised to see no instruments. They were making the sounds with their voices. She had never heard anything so wonderful. With the music started playing and tiny fairies came out into the clearing dancing around and their little wing lighting up the now darkening sky. Everyone was busy eating cake and laughing or dancing that when a very small fairy named Lilly flew into the gathering yelling out something, no one had noticed. It was hard being so tiny because no one paid much attention to her. They were all having too much fun celebrating. Tiny Lilly tried to speak to several fairies, but they just shushed her and shooed her away, ignoring her. The only one that had noticed her, was Little Marie. For a while she was content eating her yummy cake and watching the unusually beautiful scene that was unfolding before her eyes. But to her surprised, the tiny darling of a fairy that was trying so hard to get attention and so rudely being ignored, had her curious. Then she heard Lilly say, "FINE then... IF NO ONE CARES I WON'T TELL!" Lilly cried in her tiny voice, then flew into the forest as fast as she could, to Little Marie it was a flash of light. She looked around again, astonished to see that no one was paying any attention so without a thought she flew after Tiny Lily. She could see glimmers of light through the trees, but Lilly had left so fast that Little Marie could not keep up with her. Calling out did not help. Now looking around Little Marie realized she was in the dark thick forest! She tried to go back the way she had come but without Christina's stone of light that had guided them through the dark forest she was lost. She could not hear the party, either. Flying slowly now because of the darkness she landed. That's when she started to cry out for help. Without warning something jumped out of the dark and put a cloth bag over her head, while grabbing her with strong arms. Then a deep gruff voice said, "Be quiet or you are dead!" Before she knew it, she was being carried away to who knows where, by an unknown creature.

    All kinds of things started to invade Little Marie's mind. Who, why, where, & the most scary- what's going to happen to me? Fear became so loud that she could not think of anything else. She was trembling and softly crying by the time the creature stopped and threw her down to a hard wet cold floor. She tried to move her hands but found that they were tied together. All she could do was just lie there sobbing and waiting for what was going to happen next. After some time went by, she could not cry any more. She was at the end of herself, so in the quiet of her despair, she surrendered to her exhaustion. That is when Little Marie heard a voice that seemed to speak in her heart.

    "Self-Control is a seed I have planted in your heart when you first believed. You must receive it and use it! Faith is the water that makes self-control grow, if not it cannot do what I have intended it to do, to help you in times like these." First, she chose to receive this truth in her heart and then she chose to believe it with her mind. Suddenly a peace and calmness came upon her soul. She took a deep breath and then another. She called out "Who is there? Is anyone out there?"

But she heard no audible answer. Little Marie sat up as best she could, finding a stone wall to lean on to rest while she waited. Oh, that word "wait" had never brought such fear! Waiting in the dark in what feels like a wet deep dark dungeon, with no control of what is happening to you was the test of faith for sure.

That is when Little Marie thought about what she heard in her heart that brought such peace, **Self-Control**. What does that mean? How could that help now? When she thought about it for a while, she realized one big lesson, the only one she could control was her own self. But what good did it do if she chose to use Self-control when others did not? Then she thought, for one thing I am calm now and able to think again instead of freaking out as her sister would put it! That thought made her smile to herself. Now she was having a little hope rise up inside her. How could this be?

"I know you are there I AM the Son. You said you would never leave me or forsake me! But I am feeling a little forgotten here tied up and sitting alone where ever I am." She found herself saying.

Instantly the rope that tied her hands loosened and the bag fell from her face.

"I AM your Savior you shall not fear? You are my beloved and I AM with you. I will give you Love, patience, peace, kindness, gentleness, faithfulness and Self-control! These are to help you against your enemies in life" She looked up and saw a man, in white with a beautiful glowing face and bright clear eyes sitting cross legged before her.

She fell face down, finding her voice she said, "Oh my, thank you my Jesus, those are wonderful gifts." And after another moment when she could speak again, she questioned, "but I do not understand how they can be used against my enemies?" Little Marie asked looking up slightly.

Jesus reached out and picked her up to sit at his feet. "It's ok my child please look into my eyes then you will understand how much I love you. You will understand what you need to do right now for this time and this place that you find yourself in. I have given you the counselor I AM the Holy Spirit who teaches all truth and wisdom. He speaks for My Father and Myself. WE are one in thought and deed. We created everything together. Learn from Him. Trust Him." Jesus smiled "I AM always with you because He is in you!"

"Thank You so much. I will trust Him because I trust You! But how can I be sure I'm hearing Him instead of the enemy or even worse myself?" Little Marie asked remembering how the enemy Fear and Lies, tricked her and also how that man hurt, Christy and herself.

"You will need to learn My Word that has been written down for all to have access to what WE have done and said. Throughout history Our testimony has been spread in word and in deed but be careful there are those that have twisted or changed Our words, making US into their religion. So, when you read or hear My Word always do so with the Holy Spirit's guidance. He will reveal all that needs to be revealed. But do not worry right now for I have blessed you with wisdom and understanding beyond your years, my little one. Seek the truth with all you heart, mind and soul and you with find it. Do not be like those that only seek a truth that feels right to what they want to believe. I'm talking about the absolute truth that mankind is starting to forget. I AM who I AM created the heavens and the earth and all that inhabit it. I Am Almighty and My character is Love, Mercy and Grace. I am Jesus, the way provided to free you from the path of destruction." Jesus bent over and kissed her on the forehead. Placing something in her hand and He said, "Here is something to help you, for this adventure you find yourself in. When you wear it and the need arises, it will light the way. Remember I AM the Almighty and WE are with you. Now go back to the forest quickly there will be help there!" He kissed her hand that was holding the necklace. Looking deep into her eyes for a moment longer, he smiled to see such innocence still there which made his heart sing, then he raised up and walked out of the cave entrance, vanishing into the darkness.

With joy and peace flowing through her, Little Marie put the necklace over her head, and it started to glow blue. She found her way to the entrance of the cave, seeing no one, she took off flying into the forest, that was just ahead of her. The necklace shinned bright enough for her to see her way through the trees but not too bright to show her enemy where she was. As she was flying deeper into the dark forest, a tiny noise buzzed her ear and then she heard it again. "Who is that?" Little Marie asked.

Little Marie Grows Up

"It's me Lilly of the Pond fairies." The smallest of fairies rested on her shoulder.

"Thank you for coming after me. When I saw you get taken, I was so afraid for you!" Lilly said with a shiver.

"Oh my, you are welcome. I saw you were upset, and no one paid you any attention, so I wanted to listen to you." Little Marie slowed down a bit to make sure she was going the correct way.

"Follow me sweet pretty fairy. I can show you back to Christina." Lilly flickered light as she flew just ahead. Then all of a sudden Mommies voice was there.

"Little Marie wake up, wake up!" Mommy called out from the hallway. "You don't want to be late for the bus, again!"

"Wait, wait.... ah no I was dreaming!" Little Marie murmured with disappoint at that realization.

Then she turned to Christy, "Why did you let me sleep?" she whined.

"Boy what were you dreaming last night? I had a hard time sleeping with all the tossing and turning you were doing!" Christy said while she got dressed.

Still vividly remembering the dream as if it were real, Little Marie answered, "It was wonderful!" Then thinking to herself, was it real or a dream. Jumping out of bed something dropped to the rug on the floor at her feet. Before Christy would notice, she picked it up. It was the beautiful necklace Jesus gave her in her dream. She could not believe her eyes at first. Thinking twice about telling Christy, then a moment later deciding not to tell her just yet, she excitedly but quietly put it away with all her treasures she kept in a box that she hid under her bed. She decided to keep this to herself until she knew what was going on!

Well today sure started the first tests for Little Marie in the real world and self-control. Normally she would want to run and tell everyone in the house her wonderful dream, but she felt something telling her to keep it to herself. Was this the Holy Spirit of Jesus? "OK" she said to herself, "I will not tell anyone, well not right now anyway". She added

She got ready for school as fast as she ever had and caught up with her sister Christy at the kitchen table.

"Good Morning sleepy head" Mommy said.

"Morning Mommy!" Little Marie said with a big yawn.

"Mommy, Little Marie was having a dream last night! She was tossing and turning but seemed mostly happy." Christy commented as she got up from the table to put her empty bowl in the sink. She looked back to see what her sister's response would be.

"Well I hope it was a good dream?" Mommy asked with a wink, seeing Little Marie smile, she smiled too.

"Yes, it was very good, Mommy..." she answered with her dream flooding back to mind. Self-Control kept ringing in her head, as she finished breakfast. With her mind on her fairy world she ran out the door, to the bus, forgetting her lunch!

Seeing the look on Little Marie's face, Christy had to wonder to herself what the dream was about. But no time to ask now the bus was going to be here any minute and look Little Marie forgot her lunch. She grabbed it with her stuff and ran out after her.

"Wait up sis you forgot something." Holding the lunch box up to show her what that thing was! Little Marie stopped and laughed seeing her sister running with her Little Pony lunch box. Then both sisters got on the bus together, giggling.

Now normally Christy sat with her friends but she was wanting to ask Little Marie about the dream so she tried to sit with her, but there weren't two seats together, so Christy frustrated realized her questions would have to wait, so she sat down next to Misty.

For Little Marie self-control was needed everywhere she went that day. She had never given it this much thought and now that's all she could think about.

Her friends at lunch got tired of her pointing out what they should be doing or not be doing, that they started to ignore her. Stephanie finally spoke up as everyone was getting up, "You know Marie, what you're talking about is no fun and we don't want to hear it anymore!"

"Sorry!" she heard someone say as they ran off to play outside for recess.

Little Marie sat for a moment asking herself and the Holy Spirit why her friends left her there.

"No one wants to be told what to do. They need examples. Talking about controlling themselves without their Creator's help is hopeless. Do it with Us, for with God nothing is impossible." Little Marie thought out of nowhere.

Little Marie Grows Up

"Oh OK, do it not just talk about it?" That sounds right she reasoned! So the rest of the day she worked on herself not others. By the end of the day she was surprised to see she had finished all her school work and that there was no home work for her today. The teacher even gave her a gold star for listening and being helpful. It has been a long time since she had received a gold star! Some of her friends even said goodbye to her too. She went home very content and happy. Christy had a friend coming home with her today so Little Marie thought she would have time alone to try to figure out the necklace. But she was wrong because both Christy and her friend, Misty kept asking her about her dream. That it became harder and harder to not tell them about it.

"Come on I know you can remember your dream at least a little?" Christy was saying while they were walking in the door.

"Yes, you can remember, please?" Urged Misty.

"I am hungry. Maybe I will remember after I eat" Little Marie ran past them to the kitchen throwing her backpack on the floor. Finding the afterschool snacks Mommy left for them in the refrigerator, she brought the plate of little sandwiches and milk to the table.

"Hey there, you're not supposed to leave your backpack on the floor, silly," Christy called out while putting it on the hook by the door next to hers. They followed her into the kitchen. So, the three girl's sat at the kitchen table eating the yummy food. After finishing her first little sandwich, Christy started bugging Little Marie again. "Ok now you should be able to remember, come on tell us about the dream!"

"OK, OK... It was a dream about Mermaids and fairies. That's all!" Little Marie said like it was no big deal. She got up and went into the other room, but they followed her again, so she lost control and yelled "Stop bugging me. I want to be left alone!" Then she ran down the hall into her room slamming the door.

All she wanted to do is get to her necklace and look at it but she needed to be alone to do that! Waiting a few moments to make sure they were not following her, she looked under her bed to find her box of treasures. Opening it carefully she searched through the little trinkets she had collected so far in her short life. There were shinny rocks, cards with pretty pictures, and a ring Daddy had given her. "Oh, there it is." She sat back on the rug on the floor by her bed pulling out the silver necklace with a jeweled pendant.

"How beautiful" She exclaimed. It was silver with a tear drop crystal in the center of a heart. A diamond was on the top of the heart, surrounded by 12 stones Little Marie had never seen before. The right bottom of the heart had a Ruby tear drop and the left side a touch lower was a Blue sapphire. On each side of the silver braided heart were 12 small diamonds leading down to the ruby and sapphire stones. It had three chains connected to each side of the large diamond on top. Three small pearls connected the three chains into one braided loop, making a necklace. It was more beautiful than any jewelry she had ever seen and held it close to her heart for a moment thanking God. She was about to put it on, but she stopped when hearing a loud knock on her door, so she hid it in her pocket.

"Who is it?" She said in frustration.

"I'm sorry Little Marie we will leave you alone. We are going to watch TV and wanted to see if you wanted to watch with us?" Christy was really sorry and wanted her to know it.

"I'm fine! I want to be alone!" Little Marie found herself saying a bit loudly, her anger was still in too much control for her to care about Christy's feelings. When she heard Christy sigh and walk away, she crawled up on her bed and pulled out the beautiful necklace from her pocket and put it on…....

At once she was transported back to the fairy world as a beautiful fairy again! "What is going on?" She thought to herself. Looking down to see the glowing necklace hanging around her neck and for the first time she noticed a small cross etched in the center of the crystal. Then looking around she found herself at the edge of the forest, facing the clearing where the party had been.

"There you are Little Marie." Nanny came from the woods behind her. "We have been looking all over for you. Are you alright? Where have you been? Miracle saw you fly into the forest and then you were gone?" Nanny was now asking, out of breath.

"I'm alright. How long have I been gone?" Little Marie asked as she flew over to meet Nanny.

"Well let me think, it must be about three hours now. What do you think, Christina?" Nanny said looking behind Little Marie.

Little Marie Grows Up

Little Marie turned around and came face to face with Christina her Fairy God Mother.

"That sounds about right. Nanny would you be a dear and pass the good news Little Marie has been found! I would like to talk to Little Marie alone please. Thank You." At that Christina took Little Marie's hand and led her to the eastern entrance of the clearing and they entered the forest.

"I want to show you something first, sweet Little Marie. When we get there, you can ask all the questions you want, but do not tell anyone about the place we are going!" With a wink she led Little Marie deeper into the forest with the light of her staff and the light of Little Marie's necklace eliminating the way. It was a lovely path that wondered through all kinds of trees. Some were small baby trees fresh and light green; some were tall dark green arrows reaching for the sky, while others had white trunks and beautiful heart shaped leaves that shimmered different colors in the wind. They all were growing along a wondrous misty river. At places the water was a calm clear blue green, with white mist hanging low around the edges where the trees grew. But other places it flowed so fast and hard against the rocks the water was a pure white mixed with swirling blue waves that made a splashing musical sound. At the next bend in the path, Christina led Little Marie through the tree's and over the large round boulders that looked like they were piled there by a giant. There was a small waterfall flowing into a deep pool surrounded by the boulders where the water disappeared underneath, finding its way, to join the big river. It was a lovely place you could only see from the air. The boulders that surrounded it were large and smooth making them very hard to climb. It seemed a place for only the winged creatures to go. Christina led Little Marie to fly to the edge of the pool that had several very soft looking, mossy rocks placed perfectly to be fairy chairs and benches. It was the perfect place to rest for a while.

"Oh, Fairy God Mother, this is a beautiful place. I am so amazed at how beautiful this fairyland is and how I change when I'm here. Am I really here? I was awake this time so this can't be a dream. I was in my room, on my bed when I put this beautiful necklace on. Then I was in my dream again." Little Marie held the necklace out for Christina to see. "Jesus gave this to me the last time I was here and when I woke up from the dream, I was holding it. I had to believe my dream was real because the necklace was real! But now this is much more mysterious. I'm back but not where I was before? When I was here last time, I needed to be saved. I had flown into the forest after that tiny fairy Lily, because no one was paying any attention to her, at the gathering. She was very fast and before I knew it, I found myself lost in the dark forest. When I tried to find my way back, some creature jumped out from the darkness and grabbed me. I was so very afraid. It took a while for him to carry me away to what was some kind of cave. The creature dropped me on the cold wet ground, and I could hear it leave. Then I just laid there crying for what seemed like hours! When I finally stopped, I was so tired and yet I needed to get out of there! When I let go and felt empty of trying to control what was happening, I ask for help, that is when Jesus showed up. The things that bound me fell away and we talked for a while. After telling me about the gifts of like Love and Self-control, He gave me this," pointing to the necklace again, "and then He was gone." Little Marie finished her story with excitement.

Christina smiled while she said, "What a wonderful outcome of a very scary situation! It sounds like you learned a lot of things, some that maybe are beyond your youth. The I AM the Holy Spirit will help you with understanding at the needed times, like this and by using the gifts you have been given, He will produce good things in you and your life, which we all call good fruit. As you have just found out we have a very real enemy. His followers prowl around like their master just waiting to take us captive, but you have found also that knowing Jesus has set you free from them. They will always be trying to attack you mostly in your mind yet will also try in every way possible to steal your joy, hope and faith. Remember being part of The I AM's family in Jesus you have the power and victory because He won it for you and all who choose to become His."

Little Marie ponder this for a moment, "I do seem to understand some of this but it still is almost too wonderful to be true. But what else can I do. I want to learn all I can from all my experiences that I have. Mommy has told me being teachable is what makes good grown-ups! But when I talk to Mommy about Jesus and Father God, she just said I will need to go to church to find out those answers because she does not know what she believes about God and Jesus. She was surprised that I knew about Them myself. I told her that I met Them in a dream. She smiled and said that was nice and to go play in my room. I don't think she believes me!"

Little Marie Grows Up

Christina smiled with a knowing smile. "Each individual of mankind has to choose what they believe. Most do believe in some higher being or power. The one and only Creator wants to have a relationship with His creation, mankind. He made them to represent Him on Earth in His image. In the beginning God's creation had to take a second look at man and woman to realize they were not looking at God because His glory was covering them, at that time. But because they listened to the enemy's lies, they ate fruit from the only forbidden tree in the garden that they lived in. Their minds were now open to good and evil. Free will and the knowledge of evil and good, brought a temptation, they had never known. The Glory of their creator God fell away as they realized their mistake and disobedience, which was man's first sin against his Creator. They were alone and naked for the first time ever separated from their Father. Now just weak human beings that needed to be saved. Jesus stood up in heaven and said, "I'll go down and save them!" The Love of the Creator came out in Jesus's actions that day forever more. He volunteered to pay for the consequences of mankind's choices, to be independent from their creator, which causes separation from Him. He made a way for mankind to become sons and daughters, again. The Way is Jesus the only Son of the Creator and the world has a choice to believe or not. He testified about himself while teaching about the Kingdom that is Love, Mercy, and Grace. He healed the sick and lame. He even, raised the dead! The religious people killed Him because they did not recognize God in the flesh. But He rose from the grave, having victory even over death itself. Many witnessed Him for many days after that and then watched Him rise into the clouds in the sky. Those that saw and believed had what looked like fire come from heaven come down and landed on them filling them with the Holy Spirit of The I Am the Creator and Jesus the Son. From that time until now the good-news of Jesus being Gods way of love, mercy, and grace has been spread to the world. God made a way for His created beings to become dependent of Him trusting Him in a relationship. Together with Them, to live out their God given lives to experience the victory over the enemy. Yet people really like being independent and want to depend on them-selves. Which replaces God with themselves as gods, taking credit for The I AM's glory and going against all of His right, good, and loving ways. The enemy has also twisted the truth, so some people chose religion as their god. Others have made the Law what they believe but the Law separates them from The I AM and becomes their goal to prove they can do it without Gods sacrifice, trying to please God. But that is just another way to say what Jesus' sacrifice was not good enough or worse was not needed, believing they still have to do something more than just believing/having faith in Jesus as the Son. They miss the point of grace and the gift of the Holy Spirit to change them inside out. Laws and rules keep people in line, so man made a religion out of Jesus. The good news is lost to people that don't live in the freedom of grace. The law makes them judgmental, unforgiving and self-righteous which by no means represents the I AM the Creators character. While others chose to believe in idols or man-made things believing they have power. And finally, others don't want to believe in anything other than themselves. Your Mommy and sister will have to make their own choice. Your Mommy was taught religious ways, and, in her mind, God has failed her. But do not worry Little Marie it is not your responsibility to change any one's mind. They are both loved by the Creator I AM, God will make Himself known to them and they will make their choice. You just keep loving them and showing them, what Jesus looks like in you. By what you say, what you do, and how you live, with the freedom that grace brings to experience and find God's joy and purpose for your life." Christina finished, while looking into Little Marie's pretty blue eyes. She could see that Little Marie understood what she needed to for now. The rest will become clear as she grows up.

"Jesus is so amazing. He even set me free from fear, here in the wonderous place." Little Marie said thinking back to the dark cave. "I will try to do as you have said but I have to tell the truth it is not that easy. All day at school I tried to have self-control. I was proud to get a gold star and it felt good to make the teacher happy, but my friends didn't like it too much when I wanted them to do the same. Then trying to keep the dream to myself was really hard but I just knew I had to for some reason. My sister and her friend kept asking me, but I didn't tell!" Little Marie held her head up high smiling because she was feeling very proud of herself, recalling the good parts of the story.

Christina smiled then commented "So you didn't need any help? Good for you."

Little Marie Grows Up

"Well, now that you say that I did have to try really hard and then in the end I lost my temper with my sister!" With a lowered head she said. She then had to admit, "I did need help! I guess that is what you meant by people trying to live by the law to please and prove they could do it themselves. Do they always fail too?" Little Marie asked with a soul full look.

"All fall short of the glory of God. It seems to be hard for people to rest in God's love for them and trust He wants to live out life in and through them, His creation. That is how mankind can experience The Creator through giving The Holy Spirit control to work out in their hearts and lives – Love, Joy, Peace, Patience, Kindness, Goodness, Faithfulness, Gentleness, and Self-Control. Against such things there is no law." (GAL 5 22-23) Christina went on, "You have learned a valuable lesson Little Marie early in life. It is He that works within you not you alone that does anything. By you learning to rest in Him and learning from Him, the Holy Spirit, together you will produce good fruit and enjoy life. He will finish the beautiful work He starts in you. Now that's only done through each one's lifetime no matter how long or short that may be. It's a beautiful relationship The Father wants with His children." Turning toward the little waterfall, Christina pointed saying, "Come now let's drink from this little waterfall to refresh ourselves for the next part of our journey."

They both bent over and took a long drink of the clear cold running spring water. Being refreshed, Little Marie flew, not far, to the other side of the little water fall. It was so peaceful here in this special place. Hearing Christina explain about the Creator and His love for His creation was wonderful and magical to her. She saw the beauty of His creation in this place so clearly. Everything glistened with some kind of tiny light of life when it moved. All kinds of colors and shades of color where here. The water was clear at the top, then turning to the deepest of blue the deeper it got.

There seemed to be every different kind of flower that grew here between the rocks around the falls. There were pinks, purples, yellows and white. Even shades of blues that Little Marie had never seen before. Bright green ferns also grew between the rocks with every shade of green, with emerald green moss that seemed to cover everything. It was protected by giant old growth trees and large boulders that surrounded the special place Christina brought her too. She was filled with so much love and joy, that she wanted to fly around singing thankful songs to the Creator of life, the Father God, Jesus the Son and the Holy Spirit. It was a wonderful thought that the Almighty, the Creator of the Heavens and Earth would want to be in a relationship with her! She was so happy and free that she thought she may never go home!

All of the sudden a loud piercing cry came through the trees toward the North. Both Little Marie and Christina looked in that direction. "We must go Little Marie. We are needed in the woods." Christina held out her hand to Little Marie and they flew over the boulders towards the cry. It was continuing but was getting softer as they entered the forest. Little Marie prayed and ask for guidance without thinking. Christina stopped and waited while still holding her hand.

Then Little Marie closed her eyes and talked to Jesus. "I am so happy to know you and that you are here. Thank You! We need help to find whoever is crying for help? You know where and You can help us to help them. I trust in You and I love You!" She opened her eyes and asked Christina "Is that a good prayer?"

"Yes, it was perfect, but now you will need to be listening and looking for His answer." Christina said and then they waited for a moment. "Which way, Little Marie?"

Little Marie looked around then looking down noticing her necklace was glowing slightly. She turned slightly and it brightly lit up when she pointed it through the trees to the north. Smiling for a moment she took off in that direction with Christina right behind her. When she turned the wrong direction, the light would dim so with the light of the necklace they found themselves deep in the North part of the forest nearing a huge granite rock wall. They slowed to a stop when they came to the edge of the tree line.

With a whisper Christina said "This is the start of the desolate places where the enemy dwells to make his plans of attack. We must be very careful not to be seen." Christina covered the stone on her staff and Little Marie held her hand over the necklace that was glowing brightly. From the left they saw a dark figure walking back and forth in front of a cave entrance. It walked like a man but was hunched over with the heard of a wolf. It seemed to be complaining to itself not noticing anything around it.

Little Marie Grows Up

This was when another smaller rat like creature came running out of the cave crying out "Brutal come here, you big idiot. The Master is waiting for you! You know he doesn't like to wait."

Brutal just kept pacing back in forth. "I know what he is going to say and do. I don't want to see him! It's not my fault that he took so long to go see that Little Marie creature when I brought her here! The I AM showed up before him and saved her!" Brutal was yelling now but then turned and followed the rat into the cave.

This was just the moment Christina and Little Marie were waiting for, so they flew over to the face of the cliff wall and waited in between the crevasses of the rocks, for the right time to enter the cave themselves. When they did not hear any more noises from the entrance they entered quietly and kept in the dark which was very easy because there was very little light. Little Marie moved forward sensing that this was the direction to take. There were many passage ways to take so covering her necklace and peeked through her fingers to follow the light which was shining when she held it to the right. As they turned the third corner, they could hear a quite sobbing coming from inside the next right tunnel. They peaked around into a chamber that had a long wall to the left with several heavy doors lining it. This is where the sobbing seemed to come from, so they quickly flew over to one of the doors and looked inside to find several young girls huddled together in a corner. When the girls saw them, they just stared ahead with blank red eyes drenched in tears.

Little Marie flew over to them asking, "What are all of you doing here? Where did you come from?" but they did not say a word.

Christina motioned she was going to be right back and went out to check the rest of the doors. They were all unlocked like the first one with each door revealing more groups of girls varying in age from 4 to 17. All of them were in the same condition with red teary eyes, dirty from head to toe wearing filthy ripped clothing barely hanging on their malnourished bruised bodies. Little Marie met her out in the camber thoroughly shaken. "Oh, my goodness, why hasn't Jesus set these girls free like me? They need help too!" she whispered.

"Don't you see Little Marie? He has sent help!" Christina took her into the room with an older girl she had noticed trying to tell her something, but fear had stolen her voice.

"Little Marie pray for this girl, please." So Little Marie flew over to the red headed girl and touched her when she prayed "Please Jesus set this girl free to help her and to help all the rest." At once the girl started quietly speaking of how she came to be in such a place.

"My name is Emily and I was walking home from school when a car pulled up and said my mom was sick and he was there to take me to her. I believed him because I had seen him with my mom a couple of times. After a little time went by, I noticed he had turned off the main road, toward the forest, so I asked him where we were going and that's when he turned to glare at me telling me to shut up! Then slapped me hard in the face. I tried to get out, but the doors were locked and there was no way to unlock them. After a long time driving in the forest, when it was dark, he stopped and took me inside a cabin. In the back room he tied me to the bed…." Emily fell to her knees and started to cry.

Christina knelt down beside her and said comfortingly "This has been a horrible ordeal for you, and we will take the time to discuss this when we are far away from this place. We must make haste to get you and these girls set free from this prison. Can you help us?"

Emily looked up with a glimmer of hope in her green eyes "Can you really set us free? We can't leave here, or they will kill our parents and families! We have to let them do what they want to us or all will be lost!" She shrank back down with the other girls huddled in the corner. Fear and Lies hovered in this place.

"We can't set you free but The I AM the Creator Father God and His Son Jesus can! They have sent us here to help you showing you that They want to set you free, but you have to be strong enough to believe the truth from the one that created you not the lies you've been told by your enemy. With help from The I creator we can help you escape this prison you now find yourself in." Little Marie surprised to hear herself announcing.

At that statement the light from Little Marie's necklace filled the cave chambers and one by one the girls stood up. All the girls, twenty in all, gather around Little Marie and Christina at the entrance to the Chamber. With Christina at the front and Little Marie at the rear, with a silent prayer, they all quietly fled into the hallways of the cave. Always keeping to the left they found the entrance with thankfulness. Christina stopped and peered out just in time to see the back of Brutal who was pacing back and forth again in front of the opening. She was thankful to see he was still grumbling, knowing this would be a distraction but she also knew it would not be enough to get passed him with twenty girls. She looked at Little Marie and whispered, "Take them back to the gathering place of the fairies and I will meet you. I have something to take care of." Before Little Marie could protest Christina flew out to have a meeting with Brutal.

"Who's there?" Brutal bellowed out with surprise. Seeing it was Christina he stood there in shock. "What are you doing her? Where did you come from?" He demanded.

"Well I was just flying by the north edge of the forest and I heard a cry. I thought I would find out what it was and if I could help!" Christina said while flying around him, then stopping in front of him so his back was turned away from the entrance.

Little Marie saw the chance of escape and took it. Having the girls hold hands they tiptoed as fast as they could to the forest edge to hide behind the trees. When they all were safely hidden, they stopped and watched the encounter that unfolded before them between Christina and Brutal.

"You don't belong here Christina!" Brutal point back to the forest. "Go before he finds you!"

"I'm not afraid of him, he can't hurt me, besides I wanted to make sure that cry was not from you. When I saw you grumbling here, I thought maybe it had been." She then smiled and her beauty shined all about her.

Stepping back Brutal looked around and seeing nothing was amiss, he moved carefully up toward her to stand face to face, her nose to his wolf like nostrils, bearing his teeth slightly, "I don't cry out like a baby Christina, you should know that more than anyone!" with that he turned around and went into the cave.

Christina for one moment stood there looking sad but staying focused she flew into the forest after the girls finding them by surprise still just at the edge watching.

"You girls should be much further away from here by now. What are you doing just standing here? We must flee." With that she grabbed the hands of the two littlest and with all the older girls following the example, they fled into the forest. After a small amount of time they heard the enemy and his lies coming after them. The girls were scared, and fear started to take over again slowing them down. Then they stopped running to cry again, but a voice like thunder interrupted their fear.

"Be strong and courageous girls for you are being delivered from the enemy's snare. He will lie and cause pain to imprison your minds and hearts causing you to think he has power over you but The I AM Jesus, The Christ, has the keys to life and death. The power to set you free to live with strength, joy and love because He loves you all. Who can be against you when The Almighty Creator of all the universe is for you? Only fools would try that. Follow those whom He shows you love, mercy and grace through. They have His power with them." The powerful voice ended.

Amazed they all looked up and in amongst the tree tops was a large bright warriorlike angel of The I Am Creator God. He was beautiful with powerful wings, in his right hand he carried, The Word of God. When he spoke the Word, it was like a sword cutting through anything in its way. They all listened and were strengthened. Then they all began to move as fast as they could and before they knew it they were far, far away from the sounds of the enemy! The Clearing was close, and they could hear and smell the meal the fairies were busily preparing.

"We are almost there, girls. Do not be frightened by the fairy creatures you are about to see. This is a place to rest and nourish yourself for the journey back to your families. Eat and rest for here you will find peace." Little Marie was surprise to her herself encouraging them in such a grown-up way.

As the girls emerged from the forest, one by one, into the north end of the gathering place, they were greeted with love and joy. There was a fairy for each girl waiting to lead her to a place at the table, to be comforted and nurtured.

Little Marie was amazed and pleased to be part of such a wonderful healing process. She was growing up in this strange wonderful world. "I don't want to go back to the real world again. This is so amazing…. Oh no."

But Mommy was calling her back and she could not say no to the love she had for her Mommy.

"Good Bye …!"

"Well Little Beth what do you think about the story so far?" I stopped to ask being a little overwhelmed with how I found myself telling my story, the one I almost had forgotten. But there were no worries when I looked down at her smile she replied, "Oh Miss Marie, I love this story. Please tell me more."

With that encouragement I continued.

Waking Up

"Little Marie! Wake up, you have to wake up!" Mommy was lifting the cover off that she had earlier put on her little girl when she had gotten home from work. Now it was dinner and Little Marie would never go to bed on time if she slept any longer.

"I'm awake mommy, its ok." Little Marie opened her eyes to see she indeed was back home.

"I was starting to worry about you sweetheart. You were sleeping so soundly for so long. You should be well rested now. Come on and get up for dinner." Mommy kissed her on the forehead then left the room.

Little Marie looked around to see if she still had the necklace because it was not around her neck again. Worried she got out of bed and there it was just under her pillow. "Oh, thank God!" She put it away into her little treasure box under her bed and ran out to dinner with a smile on her face. What an adventure she had just had! She didn't think she would have a hard time sleeping tonight! She thought with a giggle. In fact, she couldn't wait to get back there.

"Oh, hi there sleepy head, how was your nap?" Christy teased her sister when she finally appeared for dinner. Then turning to her friend Misty, she said "My little sister still likes to take naps".

Misty just giggled. So Little Marie just ignored them and Thanked Jesus for her food and her family, then dove into her dinner of spaghetti with garlic bread and salad. This was one of her favorite dinners Mommy makes. When she stopped long enough to look around the table, she saw them all looking at her strangely.

"What's wrong?" She said while wiping her face with her napkin.

"Oh, nothing you just surprised us all with saying grace for dinner. Also, you must be really hungry sweetheart." Mommy smiled looking at

Little Marie Grows Up

Little Marie's plate which was half empty already. She then started eating also. In a few seconds everyone was eating and laughing telling about their day. Mommy was in a really good mood and was waiting for the right time to tell the girls her special news about her and Paul. But since Christy's friend was staying for dinner she would wait until bed time. With a smile on her face she enjoyed the time spent with her girls. Mommy took out some pudding for desert, when they were all done with dinner. They were all full and content.

"You girls go out to the living room and watch TV to wait for Misty's parents to pick her up. I will clean up tonight, but it will be your girls turn tomorrow night."

"Thank you for such a good meal, I had fun." Misty said to Mommy and ran out to the living room just ahead of Little Marie.

The girls were all watching TV, when a horn honked twice outside, before anyone knew it, Misty got her things together and said. "Good bye and thanks again." While running out the front door.

"Ok see you tomorrow, Misty" Christy yelled after her as the door shut.

"Who was that? Misty's parents? Oh, to bad, I was hoping to meet them." Mommy said coming out of the kitchen, drying her hands on her dish towel, then hurrying into the living room and looking out the window just in time to see Misty getting in a big dark car.

"I think so." Christy said, "They honked the horn and she ran out saying, Good Bye."

"She left so fast." Little Marie said.

"Oh ok, but Christy, next time she wants to come over I would like to talk to one of her parents first. Thank you. Well now that we are alone, I have something to tell you girls that I am really happy about and hope you two will be also." She motioned them to all sit down in the living room. The girls were looking at her with big eyes waiting to hear the news. Mommy did seem very happy.

"Well, girls, Paul and I have been talking and we thought it would be fun for all of us to take a little vacation next week for spring break. What do you think?"

Little Marie was the first to jump up and down with excitement while asking, "Where are we going?"

Christy was a little less excited but still wanted to go anywhere to get away from here!

"Well Paul has a beautiful cabin on an island with a boat. He wanted to take us there, but we will have to fly on a plane." Mommy was watching Christy's reaction not knowing if she would want to go now that she had some friends but was pleased to see a smile on her face. Mommy knew Little Marie would love to go, so was not surprised to have her jump onto her lap and hug her. They all got ready for bed excited about the upcoming trip.

After being tucked in and kissed goodnight Christy waited for mommy to go to bed then came over and sat on Little Marie's bed. "I'm so excited to go to the cabin in Washington. I hope Paul and Mommy will get married and we could be a regular family again. I like Paul, he is really nice and makes Mommy really happy not like Daddy."

"I do like Mr. Paul too. I want Mommy to be happy, yes let's try to work together to help them get married!" Little Marie giggled.

"Well we can't be obvious silly." Christy giggled too. Then gave her sister a big hug and ran off to her own bed. "We are going to have a good life after all!" Christy whispered while she rolled over in her bed and fell asleep.

Back to the Forest

Little Marie waited for her sister to be asleep for a while before she crawled out of her bed and found her treasure box. Getting back in bed she opened it and took the necklace out. Closing the lid, she put the box down next to her and put the necklace on.

She opened her eyes to see, as before, she was back in her fairy world. All of the girls were leaving the clearing with their assigned Fairy God mothers or Guardian angles guiding them. Only Christina and the forest creatures where left to clean up. "Where are they all going?" Little Marie inquired.

"Each one is going back to their homes but The I Am the Father is taking them on a healing journey from the terrible abduction they have endured, before they go back to their lives. The healing will be part of a lifelong process but knowing The I Am the Son Jesus will set them free to walk that healing out in forgiveness and love. Each will have to choose what they will believe and do. The I Am the Holy Spirit will speak through many different ways to give them the truth that you have found in The Savor Jesus." Christina smiled and then said "It is time for you my dear to have some alone time in this place that you find yourself. You are protected from the enemy, but he is very angry now that you have helped set his captives free. Be watchful, yet free because The I Am, has you covered. Go have some fun but remember to be back before the sun sets. You have all day to explore."

"Oh, thank you Fairy God Mother." Little Marie's mind was full of the girls that they helped rescue. "I will remember to be back at sun set." She replied as she watched Emily the redheaded girl with Miracle the fairy of Hope entered the forest. Deciding to follow them at a distance. She heard soft music coming that was a beautiful comforting tune and

Little Marie was drawn to the melody. As she came closer, she could she Miracle and Emily resting on a log listening to the same melody. She flew up to them slowly enchanted by the song. For a moment they looked up to see her and smiled, then they turned back toward the direction of the mysterious music. All three sat there letting the music sink into their hearts and minds. It was an orchestra of wind and string instruments that seemed to come from the forest itself. As they listen each one heard a story being told that in the end brought the healing each needed. Emily was moved to gentle healing tear's and Little Marie was being washed with a warm healing feeling and Miracle closed her eyes and praised the Creator The I Am.

When the music stopped, they all stayed where they were with a peace not one of them wanted to end.

Emily was the first to speak. "I had no idea that I was loved so much by God. I understand now how what happened to me and the other girls was not what He planned. The evil in this world has hurt and lied to people so they make bad choices because of that pain, which then they cause more pain to themselves and others. Someone needs to stop the crazy cycle. Forgiveness is the start. Jesus showed us how to forgive." Then her smile faded because the pain was still there when she remembered, "Oh but I can't forgive them like that. I remember what they did to me and it hurts so much. I am too weak! O Lord, what can I do?" She looked down and started sobbing again.

Little Marie grab Emily's hand and said gently "My sister and me were hurt by a bad man. I did not want to forgive him. I was shown that he was following the enemies Lies, Fear and Pain, he is lost. Then I was shown how I was not perfect either and I to could do bad things. Maybe not as bad as the man but still bad enough to need forgiveness too. I am trying to forgive him because I too have been forgiven but only with God's help can I do that. I do still remember the hurt and pain, but I will not dwell on bad things anymore when there are so many beautiful things to think about. I pray you can forgive with God's help too." She bowed her head and asked Jesus to help Emily.

Miracle was watching this precious scene of two that have been mistreated so badly by the enemy of The I Am and His creation, showing such grace and mercy shine from them. She was thankful for knowing

Little Marie Grows Up

The I AM is doing a mighty work in these two little ones. "I will always be amazed at how wisdom and grace can come from such a young one as you Little Marie. Emily you are healed and now you need to walk that out with your Creator God. See how He turns ashes to beauty. For now, it is time for you to go back to your family and life remembering His love and how He set you free." With that they all stood and hugged each other. Little Marie said good bye and let Miracle show Emily the way home. Little Marie had much more to explore before sunset.

"Where should I go next?" She asked herself. Then she remembered the tiny fairy Lilly. She had not seen her since the first time she followed her into the dark forest! "I wonder where she may be?" Now that she had her necklace of light, she thought maybe she could go look for her again. She also was not afraid knowing she was not alone, they were always with her.

So, she flew off toward the dark north part of the forest again. Being very watchful to not make herself noticed by anything that may be out there, she flew up higher in the trees!

"What a wonderful thing to be able to fly. I can go so much faster and farther than when I run or walk. It's a freedom that I can do both." She laughed to herself. Testing out this new ability of having lovely fairly wings, she began to fly in and out of the trees, up and down and spinning so fast she got dizzy. "Oh, this is so amazing I can be flying like I'm dancing!" out of breath she slowed to hover above the trees.

Seeing the sharp jagged tops to the enemies cave up in the distance she landed in the tallest treetops to see what she could see. Perched on top of a strong top branch she stood and looked around at the vast treetops. From here she could see all the four corners of the forest. "It's an Island!" She exclaimed. On the west side was the ocean and cove, to the east a beautiful lake by a hill then past that a waste land. To the south there was a tall mountain range covered in boulders and grass and here to the North were tall sharp jagged cliffs as far as the eye ocean. They were dark wet and dangerous where no one would dare to go. Knowing what was in those caves, far too well, she decided to go to the east and see the beautiful lake up close. Staying just above the treetops she flew toward the lake. She saw all kinds of different birds and animals as she flew. When she was very close, she veered down into the trees to spy the lake from cover.

Peering through the branches she saw the northwest shore of the lake and a very strange fox like creature walking on two legs not four. He was wearing a jacket and pants with his tail hanging out. He seemed busy making something with paw like hands. Then his ears perked up and he looked back toward the forest right at Little Marie's direction. She jumped back behind the big trunk that was beside her hoping he did not see her. Crouching down, very slowly she peeked around the tree.

"Who are you? Why are you hiding?" The fox was standing right in front of her asking her a question.

So surprised that he was right there and spoke to her she tripped on a root stepping backwards but still answering the question. "I'm Little Marie, who are you?" with a thump. She jumped back up and started hovering above the ground being cautious of this little fox. She would keep her distance until she knew she could trust him.

"Oh, how do you do my dear, my name is Mitzel, but you can call me Mitz!" He bowed and took off his curious looking hat. "I live here by the lake in the wood. I was working on something for a friend when I heard a sound coming from right here!" He stood pointing to the tree.

"Well how do you do Mitz!" Little Marie curtsied, and with a smile she asked, "Do you know me?"

"I do not know you, but I know of you. All the creatures of the forest have heard about you from the fairies!" He answered. "You are the one The Creator told us of long ago and when you came here, we were to help you! I just live over there by the edge of the lake. Would you like to see it? I am quite handy if I may say so myself." He winked his fox eye, while he pointed to a strange mossy clump of dead ferns at the back of a large fir tree. Other forest debris laid around it is camouflaging it quite well. You would not have seen the hole in front of it unless you were shown.

"Oh yes that would be nice. Did you build that?" She pointed and then followed him to his dwelling place. When they were closer it was larger than it looked from afar. There was a small entrance to a tunnel somewhat hidden by live ferns and grass. It was the width for one small person to enter. The stone stairs that went down three steps ended where a rustic wooden door await to be opened. There was a small cross craved into the top middle of it.

Little Marie Grows Up

"This is the sign that all the followers of The Creator have somewhere on them or with them, so you can know if they are friend or foe!" Mitz announced in a proud voice.

"Oh, I did not know that? Do I have that sign?" She said looking very sad.

"Yes, you do! I see it as light as day! In your necklace when it glows with a cross." He pointed again this time to her necklace.

Little Marie held the pendant part of the necklace up and saw a blue white light shaped as a cross shinning from the center of the center stone. "I never looked at it close up while it was glowing. I am so happy to wear this as a sign I am His follower!" She set it back in place on her chest and enter the now opened door to a surprisingly comfortable cottage. It had two big chairs in front of a little fireplace made of stone and mud. There was a table and four small chairs with what looked like a small kitchen with another fire for cooking.

Mitz led her to sit in front of the fire and when she did, she could see out a narrow horizontal long opening, that was like a window with no glass. It was the most wonderful view of the top of Shimmering lake that stretched to the other side. It was just above ground level and hidden from view on the outside.

"Oh, this is really amazing, Mr. Mitz. You have done a wonderful job making a comfortable place to live." Little Marie said while looking around the small dwelling. "I was wondering who is this friend you are making something for before I interrupted you?" She asked thinking she may know who it was, if it was a fairy.

"Oh yes thank you for reminding me. Let me show you." He led her back up to the front of the tree and then to the place he had been working at the edge of the water. "I have a bench I am making for a friend to rest at the water's edge. She comes here at sunset every day. I thought she might like a place to sit." The bench was made out of an old root ball from a fallen tree. It was cleaned and smoothed down to a beautiful wood finish. There was the start of a carving on the back rest. It was of the oceans edge. With cliffs and waves.

"How remarkable this is. You are very talented indeed! Your friend will love it. What is her name? Can I meet her?" Little Marie ran her hand over the smooth edges.

"UH well... I have not actually met her yet either, but I have seen her here every night at sunset for some time now. She disappears when the sun goes down. She is a very beautiful dark-haired little lady and very mysterious! So, I have not introduced myself yet. I thought I would make this bench for her and then she would want to meet the one who made it!" Mitz started working on the bench again trying not show his feelings, for he was very enchanted by the young woman he made the bench for but was not ready to show it.

Little Marie did see through him, though. But with self-control her new-found friend she did not mention it. Instead she talked about the wonderful craftsmanship of the bench ending with "You have put a lot of love into this I can tell. She will definitely want to meet you." With a wink and then continued, "Well I cannot wait until sunset today, but I hope to come back and visit. Maybe by then you will have introduced yourself to the lovely lady and then you can introduce me. It was a pleasure to meet you, Mr. Mitz." She curtsied and smiled again.

"Why thank you, pretty fairy. I enjoyed meeting you also Little Marie. I am here if you ever need me." Taking his hat with a braid of vines woven in it, off and bowed.

"Thank you, I will. Good bye" she waved and flew off.

"Good bye and The Creator bless you little fairy!" He went back to work on the carving on the back rest of the bench. Before sunset he wanted to have carved a mermaid on a rock with the waves crashing into it. Little Marie's visit helped him make up his mind to meet the Lady tonight!

Little Marie flew over to the other side of the lake to see the grassy hill that rose gently up from the few trees that out lined the lake here. She looked back over the water and could still see Mitz the fox working away on his project. She smiled to herself. "It was so nice to meet another one of the creatures that live here!" she thought. "Oh, I would like to find that tiny fairy Lilly. Oh where, oh where could she be?" She looked up the hill and remembered the waste land she saw just on the other side. Well she would stay away from that side for sure!

Then there was a splash and a giggle behind her. She turned around to see only rings in the shallows of the lake forming outwardly toward the shore. "That is strange, maybe the fish can talk too!" She flew over and landed at the edge to put her toes in the water testing the temperature.

Oh, it was nice. She waded a little deeper into the water while calling out, "Hello is anyone there?" Seeing Mitz look up she waved, and he waved back then went back to carving.

She stepped a little deeper still and the water was a clear blue with a sandy bottom. The drop off was a few more steps so she stopped. Calling out again "Hello there. I would really like to meet you if you're there?"

With another splash and a giggle, a small blond wavy-haired fairy arose from the water in a spin that sprayed water all over Little Marie. "Hello back. I am Grace the lake fairy. And you must be Little Marie. Glad to meet you again!"

Laughing at being splashed Little Marie said, "Oh yes Grace, I met you at the party the other night! So this is the lake where you live. It is very beautiful. May I swim in it with you? I do love the water and it is the perfect temperature to swim."

"It would be my pleasure to have you swim in my lake. If you need it, I have a special shell to help you breathe underwater if you want to really see my home!"

Grace handed her a coiled round shaped shell the color of a pearl. It was the size of her palm. It fit just right over Little Marie's mouth, so she dove into the water knowing how to swim since she could remember. She felt so natural in the water her Mommy called her a mermaid sometimes. Mermaid! That reminded Little Marie of something. Oh yes, it is why she had come into the forest in the first place. Before she met all the fairies, she had met Crystal the mermaid. I was going to help look for her sister, see thought but Little Marie could not remember her name. After all she has been meeting a lot of different creatures. Still thinking about the name while diving under the clear lake water, with the shell in place, it was a peaceful place swimming with the fish and seeing the underwater plants of the lake. As she was keeping up with Grace, she tried to remember the name of Crystal's sister.

Grace notice Little Marie could swim very well so she started to swim around and show her how to fly under water. Little Marie pick up on the basics and they played for a while under water. When they had swum around the lake one more time, they popped up on the west shore to let Little Marie rest for a moment.

"How do you like the lake? It is clean and clear, at the moment. I have been trying to keep it pure, but the enemy likes to dump their garbage down the river that runs by the north cliffs and it sometimes flows all the way to the lake. With all of us working together we have been able to stop most of it before it gets here." Grace pointed north.

"When I saw the lake from afar, I was drawn to come here. I am so glad I have. It has been wonderful to see where you live and meet Mr. Mitz." Little Marie looked at the north shore seeing Mitz still hard at work.

"Oh yes Mitzel! He is a character and loyal too. He has been working on that bench for days. The lady that comes to swim in the lake at sunset is wondering who he is. I have not met her yet because I want to see what she is doing here first. The best I can guess she is running away from someone or thing?" Grace saw Little Marie's expression change when she mentioned running away. "What is it my dear you looked like you've been knocked over by a fish?" She giggled.

"You just reminded me of why I'm here in the first place. Crystal the Pacific Ocean Mermaid Queen is looking for her sister that ran away. Did you know Mermaids can grow legs?" Little Marie's voice rose with excitement.

"Yes of course I do. We do talk with them from time to time. This young lady does look like she could be one but when she swims, she stays in the dark, so I have not seen if she is indeed a mermaid. Tonight, I will introduce myself and let you know." Grace smiled.

Little Marie asked Grace "Please let her know her sister Crystal loves her and wants to see her. Tell her not to worry about her father. I can't stay or I would. My fairy God Mother said I must be back by sunset."

"Then that is what you must do! I will talk with her and let Christina know the circumstances of this lady or mermaid, finds herself in." Grace said "I am glad you came. Now spin around and you will be dry enough to fly." Grace then demonstrated with a leap and a twirl, she was in the air.

"Thank you again I had a wonderful time. I hope we are also helping to reunite sisters!" Little Marie said when she handed Grace the breathing shell back to her, then spun around until she was dry.

"Good bye fairy Grace I will see you again." Little Marie said while flying away with a new purpose in mind! "I must get back and tell

Little Marie Grows Up

Christina about Crystal's sister, um, what's her name, before sunset." Flying up to the top of the trees she could see where she needed to go and also the sun was laying awfully low in the sky. She would have to hurry.

Now Christina was hoping Little Marie would be back in time to see the event. She did not tell Little Marie why she should be back here by sunset, "I guess this will be a test if Little Marie trusts me! She will be disappointed to miss this moment." She whispered to Amber Wind.

Little Marie was flying toward the clearing and was almost there when she saw the tiny fairy, Lilly, who she was looking for earlier. "Oh, I don't want to be late. Well, what am I going to turn into a pumpkin? This should only take a minute." She thought so she flew down and caught up to Lilly sitting on a tree branch looking toward the clearing.

"Hello there, tiny Lilly?" Little Marie said as she approached the dark-haired pond fairy.

"Yes, I am Lilly. What do you want?" Lilly said with a pout.

"I have been looking for you a long time!" Little Marie stated while she hoovered in front of the tiny Lilly.

"Well that's not surprising remember I took you back to the gathering. He is the One who set you free. Why are you looking for me now?" Lilly stood then started flying back and forth in front of her.

"I noticed you had something to tell everyone at the party, but no one was listening. When you flew away, I followed you, but you were too fast for me and I became lost in the dark forest." Little Marie shuttered a little at the memory.

"Yes, you told me already. It serves you right doing something without thinking about the consequences. You should not have gone in that forest alone. Anyway, I do have something important to tell everyone, but I'm still too upset to try again! They don't appreciate me and why The Creator I Am made me this way." Lilly announced.

She started to fly away but Little Marie caught her by her tiny foot and said "If you have something important to tell then you must try again, and I will help you this time. Come with me now. I'm going there before the sun sets." She looked up to see that she would be late if they didn't leave now. So instead of waiting for Lilly to agree she held on to her as she flew.

"Now wait a minute you can't do this! I'm a fairy even though I'm small. It's not fair to treat me this way!" She demanded but Little Marie was too worried about being late that she didn't stop until she was at the far end of the clearing and before she let Lilly go, she said "I apologize to you my tiny fairy friend but time was running out and I had no time to explain. I hope you will forgive me." Then she let Lilly go.

Lilly flew away so fast it was like a flash of light. Little Marie entered the clearing with a sad heart only to look up and see the sun setting and yet the clearing shinned brighter than the midday sun.

Her heart leaped for joy for the light dimmed enough to see that is was Jesus the Son standing in the middle of the clearing walking amongst all who were gathered there. As He walk by each one, they bowed and he smiled touching them with His light. Then He was there in front of Little Marie, she looked into His radiant face and she curtsied. Not being able to keep her eyes from His, she smiled. She saw His love for her, and her heart burst forth with a love she had never felt. Then she heard Him say "Marie you are my beloved and I will never leave you or forsake you." His light reached out and rested on her for a moment then He moved on.

Little Marie was filled with love, joy and peace. "I love you my Lord." Is all she could say.

Then she heard "If you love me you will follow my ways."

"Yes Lord, I will." She smiled to herself "With your help!' she added.

I stopped long enough to see Little Beth was still enthralled with the story. I was also enjoying how I was recalling it myself. Things were being remembered that surprised me, also. So, I continued.

Time to Face the Truth

Little Marie awoken from her fairy world to hearing a police siren outside her bedroom.

She jumped out of bed just as Christy did and ran to the window. They could see a flashing light reflected on the wall of the neighbor's house but could not see the street from there. Looking at each other they agreed to go peek through the now slightly opened bedroom door. The knock on the front door made them run out to join Mommy in the hall. You girls stay here I will get the door. Mommy walked to the door and checked the peep hole and confirmed it was indeed the police. She tightened the belt of her robe and opened the front door.

"Hello, Ma'am, sorry to bother you but we have a missing girl that was last seen at your address. Her name is Misty Murphy." A tall slender officer said while holding up his badge. "May we come in to talk?"

"Why yes officer please come in, I need to check on my girls first. They are in the hall wondering what is going on." She said while opening the door wider, so they could come inside. Then she closed the door and guided the officers to the kitchenette to wait while she went to get the girls.

"It's OK girls you can come join us the officers have some questions about Misty." She reached out to them as they came closer and assured them it was all right. Silently with worried looks on their faces the girls and Mommy sat down at the table while the police officers told them Misty had been missing since Monday morning, but the parents didn't report it until now, Friday.

"Our questioning of Misty's teachers and friends led us to Christy the friend she went home from school with today! It seems she has been going to school all week with no one knowing she did not go home. Mam can we ask Christy some questions?" The Female Officer asked.

Mommy looked at Christy and she could see Christy was wanting to talk to them. "Yes, but I will put my little one here to bed. No questions until I get back, please." Mommy took Little Marie by the hand and put her to bed with a kiss and encouragement "Don't worry honey we will take care of this grown up stuff. You have a good night sleep."

"Ok Mommy. I will pray for Misty and I know she will be all right." Little Marie kissed her Mommy back and rolled over to go to sleep.

Amazed at her little girl's faith and wondering where that came from, she closed the door and hurried back to the kitchen. "Ok I'm back." She walked over to the refrigerator and asked, "Would anyone like a drink of water?"

"No Ma'am, we need to get to the questions if you don't mind! Now Christy my name is officer Stacey and I need you to tell me anything you may know about Misty and where she may be. She may need help?" Officer Stacey suggested hoping to urge Christy to talk.

"I don't know where she is, but I do know she ran away." Christy looked at Mommy with a tear in her eye, then down to her now clenched hands. "Please let me explain. I helped her because her step father has been hurting her and her Mom did nothing to help her. She showed me her bruises. For the last month she had started to make a plan to run away but she would not tell me where. She said she met a nice older boy that had some money and he was going to help her. I never met him, but he drove a big dark blue car, so he must be at least 16, right?" Christy was looking at Officer Stacey when she finished.

"Why yes I hope so. Did you see the car or him?" She asked

"I saw the car two days ago when he picked her up from school and then tonight, but I did not see him. At school I was too far but I did notice his license plate had thick silver chain wrapped around it." Christy answered thoughtfully.

"Was it a plate cover holder or a real chain hanging from it?" She wanted it clear.

"One of those cover thingies." Christy replied.

"So, it was a big dark blue car with a chain rear plate cover. Did you see the numbers or letters on the plate?" She was also writing down the description.

Little Marie Grows Up

"I saw an SX and I think a number 6." Christy thought back.

"Did it have two doors or four?" The officer asked.

"Two doors. Because I did see a big yellow dog in the back seat with its head hanging out the window as they drove away, but no door for it." She said.

"Is there anything else that you can think of that might help us find her?" Officer Mindy asked her last question.

Christy thought for a moment then offered "Misty was really excited tonight and talked a lot about how things were going to better from now on and that she was going to a place she will be happy! She always talked about the ocean with the crashing waves and the miles of beach to be alone away from everyone. Then she thought no one could hurt her. I only tell you this because I'm not sure she should have trusted that boy to help her. I don't know why but I don't trust him." Christy said with another tear rolling down her cheek.

"We are so glad you told us. You may be very right she may need help, or this may also be young teenagers in love and running away. We will do all we can to locate her. Thank you, Christy, you were a lot of help." The two officers stood up to leave and turned around giving Mommy a card with the number to call if they think of any more information that would help or if Misty showed up back at their apartment.

"We will be leaving tomorrow night for spring break, but we will keep in touch. Thank you." Mommy said while she closed the door behind them.

Walking Christy to bed Mommy held on to her daughter a little tighter and said "We have a lot to talk about tomorrow but for now it time for bed. I Love you and I'm proud of you answering Officer Mindy's questions so well. Now go to bed and don't worry we will talk about this tomorrow and it will be all right, sweetheart." Mommy kissed her forehead saying "Goodnight."

Little Marie had fallen asleep praying for Misty. She didn't even think about the fairy world tonight. Her necklace safely hidden in her treasure box under her bed she slept without a dream. The next morning, she woke up to the sound of her sister getting dressed for school. "TGIF!" Christy sighed. "Yes, thank God!" Little Marie thought with a smile on her face. Then the memory of the night before and the police officers came to mind and her smile was gone.

"How did the questions go last night?" Little Marie asked Christy.

Christy sat down at their shared vanity and started to brush her hair. "Did you know that Misty's step dad was hurting her like we were hurt by that bad man?" Christy asked, instead of answering.

Little Marie got out of bed and went up to stand behind Christy and said "No. I didn't know. That must have been very scary to live at her house! Did you ever go there?"

"Yes, but he was at work. I guess he would come home late at night after drinking alcohol and came into her room. She said she tried to pretend she was asleep but sometimes he made he wake up." Christy just sat there brushing her hair with a blank stare on her face. Then she asked "Do you think all men are like that? I now know of two just in the last week. Maybe that's just what they do to girls?" She wanted to cry but she had to be brave for Little Marie and Mommy.

"Oh, know I don't think all man are like that! At least I hope not. Daddy wasn't! It does seem to be a problem for some though. I was told that people that have been hurt turn around and hurt others. If they do not forgive and get help it is a continuing cycle. I'm so sorry that Misty had to run away but maybe she will be happy now." Little Marie said with her innocence evident to Christy with her last statement.

"How can you forgive and get help? Misty told her mom, but she did not believe her. She even said Misty was trying to take her husband away from her. That's when Misty decided to run away! She had to make a plan first, though. I think that's when she started to go out with the older boy she met at the park. She didn't introduce him to anyone at school. So, I don't know what he looks like. She said he was going to take her away from here. I guess that is what they did last night. Now I wonder if I should have told Mom or someone else? I hope Misty will be OK." Christy sighed when she finished her confession.

"Oh, my goodness. That is awful. I can't believe Misty's mom didn't believe her. Do you think Mommy would believe us if we told her about you know who?" Little Marie sat on Christy's bed.

"We promised not to talk about that again! But yes, our Mommy would believe us but we can't tell her or he will hurt her! Don't you remember?" Christy asked while standing up to pace back and forth biting her nails.

Little Marie Grows Up

"I remember but I don't think he could hurt Mommy anymore, because Paul will save her." She said with a wink. "They would put that man away in jail. Right now, he can still hurt other little girls like us!" Little Marie became serious, again.

"I know, I know. Don't you think that bothers me also. But Mommy is my concern and Paul is not, always here to protect her. We can't save everyone! We need to take care of ourselves." Christy sat down again taking Little Marie's hand and said, "Please promise you won't tell her?"

"OK but I still think we should. I will let you tell her when the time is right." Little Marie agreed then looked into her sister's eyes and said "We always need to look out for others. The love of the I AM the Creator- God is for us. He will help us. We need to ask though because we have the choice to do things with Him, His way or do it alone, our way. When you want to know Him, and His love just ask Him. Then you will meet Jesus His son." Little Marie smile just thinking about Jesus.

Christy was relived Little Marie would not tell. "Ok let's get ready for school."

Nothing more was said and went to school to another surprise. First thing at school, they found out there was an assembly of the entire school to meet in the gym. It ended up being about Misty was missing and the same officers asked the student body if there was any information.

When Christy and Little Marie walked home from the bus, they looked around at the cars on the street for the first time they could remember.

"I'm hoping so hard that Misty is Ok. I feel like I could have done something more to help her. I'm going to tell Mommy today about Misty and see what see says. I think she will believe me about Misty's stepdad and mom." Christy confided in her sister.

"Oh, I think she will. Why would she not?" Little Marie started thinking, Mommy would always believe her if she was telling the truth. "I will go to bed early so you can tell her after dinner." That will be prefect she thought. Giving Christy a hug then she ran up to the open door where Mommy was waiting to greet them.

"My, my Little Marie that was so sweet of you to hug Christy like that. Come on in girls so we can start packing for our spring break vacation." Mommy said as each girl walked in excitedly.

"We are going to leave this afternoon, so we need to pack now to be ready for Paul. I have packed most everything for you, but you girls need to think about what you want to bring and pack in your backpacks."

"Oh really, I didn't know we were going so soon, that's a surprise." Christy said with a sigh, being the one that liked to know the plan first before doing anything. No surprises for her thank you, please! A pout showing her feelings started forming on her usually sweet face, but before it could take hold, Little Marie hugged her and then ran to Mommy excitedly.

"Yippee, I'll be ready." Little Marie on the other hand loved to be spontaneous and free. "I'll be ready, Mommy." And in a flash, she was down the hall to the bedroom to start packing.

"Ok, well I think I can be ready. What time is Mr. Paul going to pick us up?" Christy asked, starting to get excited about going away. She liked Mr. Paul and wanted him to be there new Daddy then maybe she would feel safer.

"He will be here at 3:30 so you have 2 hours. I packed the cloths you will need and your favorite bathing suites. This is going to be a wonderful time, girls. I hope you like Mr. Paul?" Mommy asked them both through their bedroom doorway.

"Yes, we love Mr. Paul!" They both said at the same time, then they all laughed.

"He really seems to love you too!" Mommy said with her pretty smile! "He is very excited about taking use to the Island. I guess he owns land on an Island and a big cabin. We will have to go on the boat to get to the it."

"Oh great, Cars, Planes, Boats and Cabins." Little Marie belted out with a huge laugh that made everyone laugh also.

They all were ready for Mr. Paul before he got there so they sat on the couch where Christy decided to tell Mommy why Misty ran away.

"Mommy, I need to tell you something and I hope you will listen and believe me and not be mad." Christy started with a sigh. Mommy just sat back and nodded while Little Marie sat quietly across from them in the chair. "I have known Misty since she started school last fall. I was her only friend at first because she was so shy. As time went on, we both spent time talking and laughing mostly about boys and all that stuff." Christy blushed but continued "One day she came to school with bruises all over her upper legs and arms. She showed me in the bathroom and told me that her stepfather got drunk and hurts her."

"Oh, my word. That poor girl!" Mommy exclaimed while reaching out to hold Christy's hand.

"I didn't really know what that meant but when she told me I was so mad, but also afraid for her. I told her we had to tell someone. What about your Mom, I asked her, but she said, no she would not go through that again? The last time her mother slapped her and said she was trying to steal her man. They packed up and moved here, last fall. Then she said she had a plan to get away from both of them but needed more time to get some more money together. The next week she started to show up with Chuck in his dark blue car in the morning and then after school she left with him. None of us liked him but she said he loved her and was going to rescue her from the hell she was living in." Christy had tears in her eyes when she finished and looked up to see Mommy did too.

Mommy hugged her and then said, "Oh so sorry to hear this. If you had told me sooner, I might have been able to help?" Even saying it made Mommy shiver, knowing getting involved would be very hard, also.

"She made me promise not to tell and Mom it was her choice, I think!" Christy defended herself, "but now I know I was wrong, and I should have told you because I trust you."

Now Mommy was full of pride and trying not to cry, she said "Well that is a good lesson learned. Now we must trust the police to help Misty. You told them all you know about this and when they find her, we will be here for her. For now, we need trust them to find her and we can think about our trip. Paul should be here soon."

As on que the doorbell rang, and Little Marie ran to look out the window to see Mr. Paul waiting at the door. She yelled out, "He's here!" while opening the door to let him in.

"Well, hello everybody! How are my favorite girls?" He winked in Mommy's direction and closed the door.

"We are so glad you are here. We are all ready to go. Here are our bags by the door and girls please carry your backpacks and blankets." Mommy said while hugging Christy again to assure her everything was all right. Then going over to kiss Paul on the cheek to say hello. He smiled and then they all proceeded to carry everything out to the big black SUV that Paul brought for the trip to the airport.

"This is very nice Paul." Mommy commented.

"I just purchased it yesterday. I thought and I hoped, I will be needing a larger vehicle in the near future." He said with a smile while opening the back of the new shiny Tahoe.

"Hum, New car smell." The girls said giggling, while getting into the back seat. "Look there are DVD players in the back of your seats Mommy." Little Marie noticed right off.

"We are not going that far today but when we do it will be nice to have them, right?" Mr. Paul answered the unspoken question.

"This is a beautiful SUV Paul, you have very good taste." Mommy said. Paul winked again, looking her in the eyes "I sure do, sweetheart." Mommy blushed as they started to the Portland Airport on their first big trip together.

At the airport they stopped in the area for the smaller jets and found out Paul also owned his own small jet, with a crew, who helped them into the plane to get settled in for a short hour and half trip to the small airport in Bellingham, Washington.

"So, I guess you all are wondering where we are going? It a beautiful Island in the Puget Sound called Orcas Island. We will take a boat to the cabin from the harbor in Bellingham." He held out a map with everything circled and marked for them to see where they were going

"How wonderful. It looks like a beautiful area. Oh, thank you Paul this is beyond any of our dreams!" Mommy said with love and tears in her eyes. They held hands.

Little Marie and Christy noticed and smiled to each other. They were able to forget the troubles of home and look forward to the time together, if not for just a little while.

When they landed more surprises abounded, there was a limo and a truck waiting for them. The crew loaded up the truck with supplies for the cabin and the four of them got in the Limo.

"This is amazing. Look there is room for fifty people in here!" Christy said excitedly "Well OK not fifty but a lot. Little Marie sit over here with me." She slid down the black leather seats toward the front and Little Marie did the same on the other side. Mommy and Paul sat together at

Little Marie Grows Up

the very back watching the girls as they checked out the inside of their first Limousine ride. Everyone was laughing as they pulled up to a large marina with serval small ships and yachts docked in rows along each side of a two story Victorian style building. They waited in the limo until the driver opened the door and they got on a little cart, that drove them down the docks to the left of the building. The girls were quietly betting on which boat was the one they were going to take to the island.

"I bet you it's that big white with black windows all over it." Christy motioned to the Yacht at the very end on the dock they were traveling down.

"No, I think it's that one that is sparkling with gold on it." Little Marie pointed to a beautiful white and gold Yacht just coming up on the right.

"You are right Little Marie. This is the one!" Paul announced as they slowed to a sop beside it. "Do you like it?" He asked.

"Oh yes its wonderful!" Mommy said "Beautiful."

Christy said "Perfect!" Little Marie agreed with a nod.

"I'm glad you like it. It came with the purchase of the cabin and is one big reason I bought the property. Come up and let's enjoy the last part of the journey to our destination on the view deck." Paul led them up the narrow stairs to the bow of the Yacht, which was enclosed with windows floor-to-ceiling. It was furnished with comfortable leather chairs and a couch with tables carved out of dark wood, placed around it. There was a granite bar at the back of the area not to block any view. It had all kinds of sandwiches and snacks to enjoy on their voyage to Orcas Island.

Paul opened some champagne for Mommy and him. Sparkling cider was for the girls. When all of them had a glass he made a toast, "To a safe and happy time together at La Bella Sirena!" They clinked glasses and sipped the yummy, liquid.

"What does La Bella Siren mean?" Little Marie asked first.

"The Beautiful Mermaids. It is what I called the cabin because at sunset it looks like mermaids are swimming in the cove by the cabin!" Paul winked at her.

"It sounds like a wonderful place." Mommy commented.

They all sat back and enjoyed a meal as they cruised. The sun was setting as they approached the cove as on que the pink and yellow water was teaming with jumping fish reflecting the sunset colors as they jumped. Paul was so happy that he could share this with all of them!

"Look Mommy they do look like Mermaids!" Little Marie said running up to the window.

"They are beautiful. Oh, look there's the Cabin? What? That's not a cabin, it's more like a log mansion! Paul, this is way more than you led us to believe. Most people exaggerate but you have surprised me again."

"Sweetheart I'm full of surprises! I hope you like surprises!" He kissed her hand that he was holding. Mommy looking deep into his green blue eyes. She saw something there that drew her to him like know other man had. Blushing she looked away. Paul smiled to himself feeling good about this trip and hopefully the future!

"Well, girls, we need to be ready to dock. I will be right back." Paul hurried away to talk to the captain.

Mommy and the girls stood at the front window of the ship and stared out in amazement. The "cabin" was made of logs but that was as close to a cabin as it got. La Bella Sirena stood back in the trees from the beach. Various rock walls lined two levels of grass, with beautiful landscaping that blended with the surrounding forest. The staircase was made of the same natural stone as the rock walls. They went up to the bottom stone patio which led to a wall of windows. The three stories were surrounded by wrap around decks made of small logs and more windows than they had ever seen in a cabin. Placed along the south shoreline of the cove stood three small but beautiful log cabins which they all found out later was part of the property. The staff stayed in the closest to the big cabin, the next one a guest house and farthest one was a pool house next to the dock they were pulling up to now. It was a beautiful surprise Mommy thought even though a bit overwhelming.

Paul came back and led them out and down to the dock. The lights turned on around the grounds and the house just turned on as they got into a golf cart to take them to the main cabin-house.

"This is like a dreamland. Everything is so beautiful and "big"! I can't get over that this is yours?" Mommy said to Paul with a questioning look.

"Yes, this is mine. I am an only child and my parents died when I was ten years old, so my Grandparents raised me. They owned one of the first successful logging business's in the Pacific Northwest that produced their fortune. When they retired, they purchased La Bella Sirena cove? They had the main log cabin built but the other buildings I have put in when I inherited it. This is a special place for me." He said as they pulled up to the front of the main cabin.

The inside was decorated as beautiful as the outside. They walked into the living space to see the last part of the orange sun slipping into the ocean. It was a spectacular view. Floor to vaulted ceiling windows with the second floor having a loft over the entrance to the great living room. It was decorated with the view being center stage. The large brown leather couches and comfortable chairs were arranged to take in every angle of the view. The walls had art work from the local artist colony in rich colors, with a portrait of a handsome older couple and a boy about 12 years old, standing at their side. They were all smiling looking out into the distance that at this time was the cove because the picture was hung over the stone fire place.

"The bed rooms are upstairs. The staff has placed the bags in your rooms. I hope you like them." Paul said leading them up the stairs to the second floor. "Here is the room for you girls" He opened the door to a large room as big as their apartment living room and kitchen! It was decorated for girls that like pretty things. With matching white bedroom furniture facing each other on each side of the room again, with floor to ceiling windows on the entire front wall. The view was overlooking the forest toward the cabins and dock with part of the beach in view. One bed had blues and lavenders on the comforter and Christies backpack was sitting on the chair by it. The other bed with Little Marie's bag by it had pink, orange, and yellow flowers with a touch of blue on the comforter. Everything in the room looked well put together and thought out. Again, Mommy was taken back by the beauty of this place.

The girls ran in and looked at the room excitedly. "Your Mommies' room is right next door with the connecting bathroom." Paul opened the door to a Jack and Jill bathroom that had a soaker tub with a window with the view of the cove. They followed Paul through to what would be Mommies room.

"Oh, how lovely, Paul. These are exactly my colors! It is done up like the beach cottage I always wanted." She smiled at him.

"Ah… we will get ready for dinner." Christy announced as she pushed Little Marie back into the bathroom and closed the door. Whispering to Little Marie "Lets them have some time alone. Can you believe this place! It's amazing." They went back into their vacation room dancing and giggling.

"It is wonderful." Little Marie chimed in. "This place reminds me of a place in my dreams!" She said then stopped, realizing she might give away her secret, so she changed the subject. "Do you think Mr. Paul will really want all of us? I mean if he marries Mommy, he has to take us also, right?" She got a worried look on her face thinking of the alternative.

"Of course, silly. Do you think he would bring us here and have these wonderful rooms for all of us if he did not like us too!" Christy said trying to convince herself she was right.

"I think you're right. I really like him, and did you see how Mommy looks when she looks at him? She gets all pink and nervous." Little Marie said with a giggle.

"I know it's funny but that's what they call blushing and when a woman is with a man, she loves that happens, so I think she loves him!" Christy declared.

"How do know about blushing. Do you have a boyfriend?" Little Marie teased her sister.

"No, who would like me? Anyway, I like watching those movies with Mommy about love and romance. You are always busy playing with your dolls or something, so you have missed them." Christy was no way going to get into boy talk with her little sister.

"Oh, those movies are too mushy, and I don't like that stuff. You and Mommy can have your movie time. I have my times with Mommy too!" Little Marie said a bit defensively.

"Yes, you do, so no problem, I was just answering your question. Let's get ready for dinner and maybe we will have some time to explore before we eat." Christy walked over to her little sister and hugged her. "We are going to have a great spring break."

The girls cleaned up and then went down stairs noticing Mommies door was closed.

"Well I think we have some time to explore let's go out to the backyard. It is lit up so nicely with white lights. I saw them come on a minute ago." Christy said, and they ran down the stairs and found the back door to go explore.

Behind the closed-door Mommy was talking with Paul.

Taking A Break

"Well Beth, I think we need to take a little break, looks like a good time for a nap." I whispered, seeing she was dozing off already. I put a blanket over her and told Buddy to stay, so he laid down right next to her. Looking down at the small face sleeping there I thought life is sure full of surprises. Who would have thought I would be telling my child hood fairytale to this precious child that has been mistreated in ways still not known?

With Beth napping on the couch with Buddy, curled at her feet, I went out back to take in the beauty of the lake that was reflecting the colors of Fall. Still thinking how meeting Paul was one of the best things to happen to my mom and us girls. Remembering the day, he had purposed to her, was a story in itself. She had fun retelling it to me the last time I visited the island.

She said very dramatically as she remembered saying to him, "Oh, Paul this is so wonderful. I am so happy." While she was looking out at us girls run down the grassy grounds of Paul's amazing place. "I've never been to a place like this." She stopped talking because Paul came up behind her and swung her gently around to have her end up in his arms!

Looking her into her eyes with their lips almost touching he whispered, "You don't know how much I wanted to hear those words from your beautiful lips. I want to make you happy." He then kissed her deeper than he had kissed her before. She was overcome with passion and joy at the same time. She blushed at telling me. "He is a romantic you know!"

Paul declared between kisses His love for her, adding she was a dream come true!"

Little Marie Grows Up

She said she melted into his arms forgetting everything. Time seemed to stop until a loud scream came from the backyard! It was in the direction of the cove. I told her that is when I fell in love with Paul as a daddy. We laughed together at that confession. Well he was there to rescue me and ultimately all of us.

My cell phone started ringing at that thought. "Hello. This is Marie."

"Hello Miss Marie, this is Special Agent Manchester with the FBI. I have just arrived at your office and was told you were detained with one of the new comers?" The man said, with a very authoritative voice.

"Good afternoon Agent Manchester. The answer to your question is, well, yes and no. I am available, but would you have Jenny bring you to the cabin by the lake? I will explain when you get here." I was hoping to not disrupt Beth's time of rest by taking her back right now. He agreed and said he would be their shortly. This brought back to me all the anxiety regarding the voicemail threat. What timing when I am having a break-through with little Beth and I had to admit with myself, also. Yet I am glad they sent someone to look into the latest call. Maybe I can get this new agent to handle this case once and for all. It has been over 25 years and they have not caught this SOB. Now that the "the Boss Man" has raised his ugly head, admitting to Sam's murder and his evil plan for revenge against me. This is the time he must be stopped before anyone else gets hurt. Realizing I had been pacing angrily at my thoughts, but still wanting to change the directions those thoughts were going, I looked into the cabin window, happy to see Beth still napping.

Saying a little prayer, I calmed myself by remembering the tale I had been telling Beth, my little girl experience. Self-control is a curious thing that we all take for granted after we get to a certain age and if we have learned to be a happy functioning adult in society, we use self-control all the time. It is times like these I am amazed how it is a choice to use it or lose it, as I have been known to say from time to time, because if you don't use it you will lose yourself to fear and become a person never at rest or peace. We all need to control our thoughts or we they can drive us crazy. Peace is what I have been hoping for, for a long time now. I guess you could say since my child hood looking back now. I have found it many times, but it is always being tested as it is right now. Fear is knocking at my door and I have been very tempted to let him in.

But I must refuse his voice and turn to the voice that has always been my peace. Jesus! Again, I prayed with determination to keep my focus on Truth and the Light that overcame...

"Excuse me, Miss are you, Marie Underhill? Oh, so sorry to..." Special Agent Manchester walked around the corner, closer to where I was sitting, but his voice trailed off, for some reason.

"Looking up I saw the flash of his FBI badge and knew who he was. "Oh yes, Special Agent Manchester I am guessing? Where is Jenny?" I stood up to go shake his hand. He was a tall, dark haired, handsome man with a beautiful smile. I could not help but smile back. Did he just blush, no that must be the lighting of the day.

"Why yes, that is correct, Manchester, at your service." He said clearing his voice. Reaching out to shake my hand as if he was confirming I was real. He then asked, "I hope I did not alarm you? Miss Jenny went in the cabin and I came around back to look for you."

Having to tilt my head a bit, I answered, "Well looks like you found me. Please, let's talk out here, if you don't mind. That way we will not wake up little Beth, that is resting inside." I motioned toward the lake and the fire pit with Adirondack chairs to sit in.

"That is a good idea Miss. Underhill. Miss. Jenny filled me in on the three new girls that have arrived this last week. Also stating you have the youngest one here, because she ran off?" He asked with a more professional tone. Getting out his note book made him look very FBI'ish, whatever that means.

With a smile at that thought I replied, "Special Agent Manchester, please call me Marie. I am so glad you are on the case and I really hope you can help solve it. This has been going on far to long! Now, to find out about Sam's murder not accident, plus the threat of more to come, is very unnerving to say the least. I feel safe knowing the island is a safe place, but I do not want to always have to stay here, making it a prison in away."

I sat down across from him. He looked up from his note book and smiled. Wow that smile is perfect on his masculine face. He is way too good looking for me, so I didn't want to give it a second thought. But it was sure nice to have a strong man on the case, being handsome was only another plus. I replied, "To answer your question, yes, Beth ran off. She has not talked much to anyone yet but seemed to trust me. I found her in the woods hiding and I coaxed her out by telling her the story of when I was a little girl. The time when I helped find the first eighteen girls that were kidnapped. She liked it so we came here to rest and finish the story."

Smiling he said, "Well Miss. Marie, I am here to help solve this case and catch this creep. With your help, again we might just do that. It is good you started remembering because we will have to talk about what happened back then until now to try to track down this criminal! This might take some time and I would like to start as soon as possible. The last call makes me think he is close, and we need to be on guard. I will call for reinforcements if needed but I will need to report my conclusions first to decide if we need to get the back up. Special Agent Green has briefed me on what her investigation has turned up and what happened that night when you were eight years old. You seemed to have information that was very helpful but somewhat strange to say the least." Special Agent Manchester said with his FBI voice getting back focused on the case.

"Yes, I can see why you would say strange. I had not remembered those dreams and the island for a very long time now. Timing is everything I have found, so I do believe we will find this SOB and he will not hurt anyone else! I swear if he ..." I stopped. I just could not say out loud what I wanted to do when we catch him. I looked out to the other side of the lake trying to avoid Manchester's concerned looked. "That's funny. Something moved out there? It must have been a deer. They come down to the water just before dusk. Um wonder why it ran off?" I said changing the subject if but for a moment.

"Where, On the other side there?" He pointed in the direction I was looking, while having me get low to the ground and behind him.

"Yes, but as I said it probably was a deer."

"Are you sure? We better go inside and check on the others. We need to be in a secure area to talk, anyways." He sounded a bit too concerned.

"To my knowledge this island is very secure, and I should be able to go anywhere safely?" I said pulling away from his hand that had grabbed my arm trying to pull me towards the cabin. "Why are you doubting the security?" I asked looking him square in the eye.

"I will explain that when we get inside. Now are you sure it was a deer? Why did you think it was a deer?" He asked again, while moving us toward the back door of the cabin.

"It was to tall to be another kind of animal and I think I saw tan looking hide going into the trees, but it was shadowy, so I am not completely sure, now that you have put a doubt there!" I was not happy to think we all could be in danger. "I need to talk to Misty our Mayor, as soon as I can to alert her." I told him as we entered the back door.

"I already briefed the Mayor, before coming out here. She is already putting the community on alert. I am going to take a look over on that side of the lake while you stay here with Jenny and little Beth, and oh yes Buddy here!" He said and bent over to pat the head of the hound dog that was now sniffing his crouch.

"Buddy come here! Sorry about that. Ok that sounds great. I feel a lot better knowing everyone understands to be careful. So, I thought Buddy and I could come with you while Jenny stay's here with Beth, until we get back?" Grabbing the leash to go without waiting for a reply.

He stopped me. "No. I want you to stay here with Buddy, Jenny and Beth. Wait here and I will be back. Be ready to go back to town when I get back. Lock the doors!" He replied abruptly, then and walked out the door.

Well that was a little rude. Oh well putting the leash down I walked over to lock the door. Then turning around, I looked straight into, two frightened faces.

Jenny was first to ask, "Is everything alright?" She then whispered so little Beth would not hear, "I'm a little scared being out here in the woods. I would like to be back in town!"

"Oh yes everything is alright. I just saw a large elk on the other side of the Lake and Special Agent Manchester wanted to see it." I answered with a calm voice. Taking Jenny by the hand I led her to the couch to sit by little Beth. "You two sit right there and I will make some refreshments, I can finish my story I started telling Little Beth?" That seemed to calm Beth's concerned look and Jenny smiled.

Little Marie Grows Up

"I will help you." Jenny joined me in the small kitchen while Buddy curled up with Beth again on the couch. "Oh, Miss Marie, I really am scared. I overhead the agent guy telling Misty to alert the coast guard to be on the lookout for boats in our general area. Do you think the caller guy knows where we all are?" Her voice was shaky.

"It will be Ok, we need to stay calm and work with the "Special Agent". Please help me keep Beth calm and we will go back to town as soon as Agent Manchester returns. I am guessing he will be back right before it gets really dark. Now here can you please bring this out and I will bring the drinks.

"Yes Miss. Marie. I will trust you like I always have and thank you again for everything you have done for me. You are a beautiful person inside and out." With a hug first then a wink she grabbed the snacks and walked to the couch.

I was starting to think I needed to look for something, but I just couldn't remember what it was. Oh well I went in to close the blinds and turn on a few lights. "Now Beth where were we in the story?" I sat down next to buddy and took a sip of water.

"Well let me think, Oh, I think it was when the sisters were going to explore while Mommy and Paul were talking." Little Beth said excitedly, then turning to look at Jenny, "Oh, Miss. Jenny this is a story about Little Marie and her sister. She has a necklace that when she puts it on, she falls asleep and is then in a Fairy world. Jesus was there too!" The little girl did not seem like the withdrawn girl that had run into the forest hours earlier.

"Well that sounds like a wonderful story. I would like to hear it too." Jenny responded with a smile.

I was sitting there amazed Beth liked the story so much, but then at the mention of the necklace, I was reminded of what I need to look for when we get back to town. I didn't even know where to begin though.

Happy to comply to the request I said, "Ok that is a good place to start." With the memory of my first daddy moment with Paul popping in my head. I started up the story again, hoping it will help me remember were that necklace went all those years ago.

When Mommy and Paul heard a scream from the cove, they ran outside together to find out what was the matter.

"Are you alright? What are you looking at? Who screamed?" Mommy exclaimed breathlessly as she came to stand next to them to see what was wrong.

"Sorry Mommy, Little Marie screamed when she found this dead bird on the beach. We are fine. But look!" Christy answered pointing to the dead seagull.

"Sorry Mommy I just was surprised. I was running on the beach and tripped over this poor dead bird!" Little Marie explained grabbing Mommies hand.

"That is alright Little Marie I would had been surprised too." Paul said bending down to console her. He then picked Little Marie up and put her on his shoulders. "I'll bring you back to the house to change your shoes and have one of the staff take care of the bird." They went back up the steps arm in arm to the patio.

Paul let Little Marie down by the back door to take her shoes off. Then announced with a bow, "Come my Ladies dinner awaits." Little Marie was enchanted by Mr. Paul.

Dinner was delicious and afterwards the girls thanked Mr. Paul and said Good night. It had been a long day! The girls where tired but too excited to sleep yet. So, they sat on their beds and talked about the trip and how nice everything was. Christy then said, "I hope that we are not dreaming?" She giggled.

"Oh, we're not dreaming, see I can pinch you!" Little Marie ran across the room to jump on Christy's bed and pinched her.

"No, no I'm not dreaming, I know…." Christy laughed and tickled Little Marie back.

Finally, they stopped laughing and were exhausted. "We should get to sleep before Mommy tells us too. Love you sis." Christy said.

"Ok. Love you too." Little Marie agreed walking back to her bed she realized she was very tired. She also had not thought about her necklace all day and fell asleep before remembering, she had packed it in her backpack. The next morning, she woke up with a jolt before the sun had come up or anybody else in the house. "What was that?" She thought. But there was nothing. It was very quiet. She listened for a moment but again nothing. "Oh well, I can…. I can't believe it, I missed my fairy world last night. I still have time! No one is up yet." She quietly got out of bed *and looked for her necklace, all the way at the bottom of the bag. "Ohhh where is it. I know I put it in here." She searched quietly and then finally found it. "Whew, there it is. I need to pack this more careful next time." She thought and laid back down in her bed while putting the necklace on.*

"Hello, hello where is everyone?" Little Marie found herself alone on the beach where she had met Crystal, the mermaid. Now looking around more closely she thought it looked a lot like La Bella Serena cove. She flew up to the edge of the forest and this is right where the Cabin would be in her world? "This is really strange" She flew in a circle... "This must be my fairy world because I have my beautiful wings and can fly, but this is so much like the cove without the cabins and dock. This is amazing! Where is Christina and the others?" She Flew into the forest with her necklace lighting the path before her. Slowing down Little Marie paid more attention to her surrounding this time. "Yes, I remember this place. This way will lead to the clearing where the fairies gather." But when she got there, she found no one and worse there was no sign they had ever been there. Even the grass was standing up were the tables and chairs had been. She flew around the edge of the clearing slowly listening to hear anything that would tell her where everyone went. It was eerily quiet. The sounds of the forest were all she heard. The river yes maybe I will find them at the little waterfall. She flew through the trees along the Misty River, over the boulders and found the lovely calm place her fairy God mother had shown her. No one seemed to be there either! "Oh no, what is going on. Where is everyone?" Little Marie said out loud in frustration.

"I'm here!" tiny Lilly popped out from behind a boulder. "I've stayed behind to see if you would come back?" Lilly snickered and landed by where Little Marie had stopped to wonder.

"Why do you laugh at me?" Little Marie demanded.

"Oh, I'm not laughing at you Little Marie. I just won a bet I made with Mitz. He thought you would not come back because life in your world is so distracting and if you grow up to fast you will forget us and this world! Well I said you were too curious not to come back and here you are! He owes me some carved furniture for my house!" Lilly laughed again shining bright colors as she did.

"You have very lovely color when you laugh." Little Marie had to smile too, but not for long. "What has happened? Where is everyone?" She asked while looking around.

Lilly flit back and forth in front of Little Marie, and announced, "They are all hiding in their homes and preparing for the next step in the battle. The enemy is furious after the escape of the girls in the cave. He has all his followers out looking for them and tormenting anyone or thing that has to do with their escape!" Lilly announced with courage.

"Oh no, then I must run away and hide too. Maybe I should just take this necklace off and wake up?" Little Marie cried while she tried to pull the necklace off so she could wake up.

The chain of the necklace was stuck in her hair and she could not take it off. "Oh no, Oh no! I must wake up and get away from here!" She started to cry.

"Why are you crying my child?" The calming voice of Jesus floated around her.

She instantly looked up and found herself sitting in the lap of her loving Savior. "Well I was scared that…" She stopped and smiled not wanting to finish because she knew how foolish fear was when she remembered The I Am the Creator is with her. "Thank you for being here. I want to wake up and the necklace you gave me will not come off." She said hoping He would help her take it off.

"When the time is right it will come off. We still have things to show you here in your dreams. This is a time to be very aware of your surroundings. Patience will help you with what comes next. Patience is your friend. He can help you with hard decisions in your life. Count to ten to give you time to remember Me. He helps wisdom play out Our plan in your life. Now go with strength and courage. Christina your guardian will be waiting for you by the path to Shimmering Lake. Peace be with you my child. Remember I Am always with you." Jesus held her tight for a moment longer than He was gone with Little Marie energized by His touch.

"Lilly will you come with me or stay?" Little Marie asked as she started flying slowly toward the path Christina would be waiting at.

Little Marie Grows Up

"I will go ahead with you but my purpose here is to spy on the enemy and what is happening and report back to the leader which for now is Christina!" She said with a bit of sarcasm.

"Well, suit yourself. I must hurry because someone might try to wake me up real soon and I want to finish what I'm supposed to." Little Marie didn't know why Lilly could bug her so much.

"I thought that's what you wanted to do is wake up and go back to your Mommy!" Lilly snicker.

"I was letting my fear make me forget who I am, because They are with me. I can do what needs to be done. If God is for me then who can be against me!" Little Marie announce and flew toward the path Jesus told her about wondering where that statement came from. Believing what she had said she moved forward being cautious and aware of her surroundings as she did so. Things where quiet and still so she was able to hear in the distance several creatures thrashing about the bushes just ahead. She stopped and flew up to a large branch that she could hide to watch them pass by.

"Ah you are a curious one" tiny Lilly said already there to watch the weird creatures below. This is a good place to spy for you, but I can get much closer!" Before Little Marie could whisper a response, Lilly flew down the truck of the tree and then hoovered just above the bottom branch that hung over the path the thugs where headed down. Little Marie bit her lip so not to cry out for the tiny fairy that was so close to where they were standing, she might be caught. Then she could not see Lilly at all. "Where did she go?" She thought keeping quiet. To listen to the thugs.

"This is so stupid! I think we should just hang out and let someone else find the bosses girls!" One of the creatures that had a pig face on a beaver body, grumbled.

"No way pig face, I want to get the reward and make the boss happy!" The creature with the beaver face and pig body said.

"Pig-face and Pig-butt be quiet. I'm tired of you two grumbling and arguing." The third creature bellowed as he came into view. He stood over the other two. "I have to find them! So be quiet and keep looking!" He pushed by them and they followed making their own path through the trees. It was Brutal the brut Christina had talk to when they rescued the girls. As they went Little Marie saw Lilies tiny spark of light from tree to tree, as she followed the three into the forest. She was a good little spy.

Little Marie went the other way and came close to the path to the lake. She slowly looked around and saw Christina standing by the tree where Mitzel's house was on the bank of Shimmering Lake. She flew happily to where she stood and hugged her. "I'm back and here to help!"

"Oh, my goodness, you are a sight for sore eyes Little Marie. Here let's go into the house to talk my dear." Christina led her into the little underground hut. Mitz was waiting to greet them at the door.

"Welcome please make yourselves comfortable." He led them to the little fire place where they could sit and talk. Then he went back to the small table where he was working on a very small bed frame the held a half of an acorn shell with cotton stuffed in the shell. It looked like a four posted bed for a tiny fairy.

Now it was Little Marie's turn to giggle. "So, you thought I would grow up too fast and never come back? Well sorry but you lost the bet!" She laughed as Mitz held up the fancy little bed.

"Well it's not that bad I lost. I really hoped you would come back, and I do like making things!" He smiled to himself proud of his little creation. "Now you two need to talk so I will go up and keep watch." He took his hat and out the door he went.

"Yes, we do need to talk. Time is growing short so listen and remember my dear." Christina leaned close to Little Marie and whispered three things to remember. "There is an evil in your world, like the enemy in this one, that preys on the weak and innocent. You have already experienced it and have been chosen to help those trapped by it because you have believed and received The Lord Jesus. Forgiveness has set you free and your testimony will do that for others. Remember these three things to help you find the ones that need to be found.

1. Faith in Him who is The Almighty Creator I Am God and His Son Jesus
2. Hope because His victory was completed on the cross. It is finished!
3. Love is why He created you and paid the price for you.

Little Marie Grows Up

"I will remember! Faith Hope and Love! Yes, Ok, but what is happening?" Little Marie still inquired.

"There are girls just like the ones we helped here in your fairy world that need help on the Island you are staying at with your Mommy and sister Christy. With the help of The I Am the Holy Spirit you can help them. Now you must remember, or they will be lost." Before she knew it, she was being woken up...

"Hey Little Marie, where did you get that necklace. Wake up I want to see it!" Christy was sitting on Little Marie's bed holding the necklace in her hand when Little Marie opened her eyes.

"What, oh no give me that." Little Marie sat up and grab the necklace back. "That's mine give it back.

"No problem, I just wanted to see it. It's beautiful where did you get it?" Christy let it go and got up to look out the windows.

"I'm sorry I just don't want to lose it. I ah found it a long time ago so ah I don't know who's it was so I kept it?" She put it back in her back pack and walked over to look at what Christy was looking at.

They saw two men walking from the dock to the pool house with a dark-haired girl walking ahead of them.

"I wonder who that is? Do you see there was a girl with them?" Little Marie asked in a concerned voice.

"I guess they are friends of Mr. Paul's." We need to hurry and get down stairs for breakfast, Mommy said we need to be down ASAP." Christy ran over to her closet and got her clothes for the day.

Little Marie peeked around the curtain so they could not see her, and noticed the dark-haired man push the girl in the door, looked around-stopping for a moment seeing the light from their window but then went into the house as if not seeing Little Marie or Christy (she hoped). She closed the curtains when she saw the door close behind the man. Getting dressed as fast as possible, the girls together ran down the stairs to the dining room to see Mommy and Paul sitting there quietly talking and holding hands.

In the Pool house, "Smithy, get her in there before anyone see's us. Paul has brought guests here and we need to get everyone hidden. We almost have enough to ship. The boss wants an even 20, so we only need one more. Damn Paul, had to pick now to come here." The tall dark hair man said to the short burly bald man wearing a black cap to keep his head warm.

"Look I have told you, Burt, Mr. Moneybags has been getting this place all fixed up for this company. I just didn't know when 'cuz I've been a little busy getting #19 to the port this last week! So back off. We have a really good hiding place where all of them are except this one. The boss might have to take the 19 now and come back for the one unless there's a miracle and a young sweet girl just shows up at our door step." He looked back before closing the door and thought he caught a glimpse of movement in the main house upstairs bedroom which happens to look right where they were. He closed the door not saying a word to the other man. He would check it out before getting Burt upset again.

"Oh, there you two are, please come join us." Mommy smiled and pointed to the chairs in front of them. "We hope you had a good night's sleep?" She asked with a twinkle in her eye.

"Yes, we slept well. How about you two?" Christy responded before Little Marie.

"It was a very nice evening." They said in unison, then laughed. "We have something to ask you girls." Paul said. "I, I mean, we wanted to know how you girls would like it if we all became a family?" Paul continued, "Well I mean, I asked your Mommy to Marry me and that includes you two girls. She said yes but I now need to have your answers but first do you have any questions for me?" He finished glad to see the girls both break into a smile.

Little Marie jumped up and ran into Mr. Paul's arms and sat on his lap. "I would be very happy to be a family! Christy and I were hoping you would ask us!" She winked at Christy.

"Yes, we were, and I would be very happy to be a family. Ah Mr. Paul." Christy came up and hugged Mommy.

Little Marie Grows Up

"You can call me Mr. Paul for now but I am hoping you two would be able to call me Dad, someday." Paul said hopefully.

"Yes, we will be a family and there will be some changes to come but all for the best." Mommy reassuringly said. "We will need to have a family meeting and discuss things but for now we are going to explore this beautiful island and have some fun today. How does that sound?"

"That sounds great!" The girls agreed.

After finishing breakfast, they put on their sweaters and went out for a walk. The morning breeze was crisp, but the warmth of the sun was already heating up the ground. On the walk they decided to have a picnic on the beach that afternoon and go swimming in the cove. The girls ran up ahead every once in a while, laughing and giggling while the adults walked hand in hand talking about the future and how wonderful it was going to be. They were already becoming a family. Little did they know they were being watched through the trees.

"Hey Christy, do you think we can get a puppy? Where do you think we are going to live? Here? I wonder when they are going to get married? Isn't this so wonderful" Little Marie swirled around and then skipped down the path while asking her questions.

Christy just smile to herself waiting for a chance to answer the first question Little Marie asked before answering the other four. "That would be fun to have a puppy, but we will have to wait to find out where we are living and no, I don't think it will be here. And yes, this is very wonderful. We will have someone that can protect us and maybe move away from that man. Even though I will miss my friends I don't like where we are living. It has become a scary place you know!" Her smile was gone remembering the neighbor man with a gun.

"Yep I think it will be nice to live somewhere else too!" Little Marie agreed as she slowed to a walk again. "Well we should write down some questions to ask at the family meeting. Oh Christy I thank God for giving us a Daddy again!" She wanted to change the subject.

"Well I don't know if I would call him Daddy, but he will be a good step dad I think." Christy somewhat agreed.

They continued down the path that led around the front of the house then toward the other cabins and the boat dock. The girls waited at the cross road of the path.

"Which way?" Little Marie asked. Looking to the left the path looked like it went away from the cove and into the forest which looked very familiar to her.

"Turn right sweetie we will go look at the other cabins. The other way takes you into the Old Growth forest and you can get lost in there very easily so that is out of bounds unless I go with you!" Paul announced, feeling like a father at the moment. Then realizing he may be over stepping his bounds he added "Just so no one gets lost, Ok?" He looked at Mommy and she smiled her agreement. "Good idea girls. We don't want anyone getting lost." Then hand in hand they turned right and approached the first cabin where George, and his wife Martha, the cook and house keeper's home, while they worked for Paul.

Back at the pool house. The short guy was saying, "Hey come in Burt, Mr. Moneybags and his guests are out taking a walk and are just passing your cabin right now. Just FYI stay low, but I think that miracle happened! #20 just walked by." Smithy spoke into his walkie talkie hoping Burt still had his turned on.

"Roger that. I am watching them right now. Over and Out!" Burt acknowledge Smithy. What a break, he didn't want to tell the boss they were one short. Now to figure out how to do it without being caught?

After the happy group finished the grand tour of the beautiful grounds, they went back up to the main cabin to get ready for their afternoon at the cove. Paul excused himself to go take care of somethings before they went on the picnic. Mommy told the girls to get their bathing suits on and pack what they want to bring to the beach, in their backpacks. "We will leave in an hour or so you girls can play or read before we go." She kissed their foreheads, then went up to her room to get ready. She packed the towels in her beach bag making sure, to bring the sunscreen.

"Hey, wait for me!" Little Marie called out running up the stairs behind her sister Christy that had started up to get her bathing suit on.

"Ok but hurry up." Christy said stopping long enough for Little Marie to run up past her giggling. This sure was starting out to be a nice vacation! She smiled to herself.

"What are you going to do for the next hour?" She asked walking into the wonderful room that they were staying in, oh that's right we can stay here any time! Now we are a family! She remembered, "this was the start of becoming a family with Mr. Paul." She thought to herself.

"I think I will take a nap." Little Marie smile to herself as she looked in her backpack for her necklace.

"What's with all the naps sis?" Christy was surprised but then thought that's fine I will have some quiet time. "OK, I'm getting ready for the afternoon." Christy said and went into the bathroom.

Little Marie had wasted no time to get changed into her pink bathing suit and cover up before laying down with her necklace on. When she found herself in her fairy world again, this time it was stormy and dark.

"I wonder if Amber wind is causing this storm?" She said entering the forest that provided a little protection from the wind and rain, but the trees were cracking and bending from the storm. "What going on. Is anyone here?" Little Marie called loudly.

"Yes, I AM, Little Marie." Jesus answered from down the path ahead of her. "This is a very stormy day. This is not Ambers doing. Please follow this path to safety my love." Jesus came closer and the storm around them calmed.

"Oh, My Lord, thank you for being with me always. I must try and remember that." Little Marie smiled at Him. "What is happening? The last time I was here everyone was hiding!"

"The enemy is prowling around roaring and bellowing. He is very upset we have messed up his plans for those precious girls, he had stolen. Do not be dismayed Little Marie for I AM with you and have already prepared for this day so trust me to deliver you from the enemy and his evil schemes. You will have to be strong and brave. If you trust Me you will have peace. You will see My strength and it will be your joy." Jesus then bent down and kissed her forehead, "Go My child time is short." Then the I AM the Son was gone.

Little Marie felt a power go into her when He kissed her but took no time to think about it because the storm was raging around her again.

Looking down the path He told her to take she could see that it was narrow dark and winding. "Ok Lord I will follow you." She focused on the path ahead with the light from her necklace glowing just enough to guide her but not too bright for the enemy to see. Just around the next corner she found Christina and Amber Wind waiting for her.

"Oh, praise the Great I Am, you made it. Come Little Marie we need to go hide for a bit." Christina hugged her then they all flew off into the dark forest until they found two trees on each side of a small clearing that just grew sideways, almost on the ground, towards each other than straight up at the point where they touched. The branches grew straight up on the side of the tree trunk that was facing up and then mingled together into the sky. It was almost like a forest fortress to hide behind. They flew over and through the branches with ease to find an old abandoned cottage hidden behind it.

"Did those branches just make room for us?" Little Marie asked noticing several times the branches moved but not from the wind.

"Yes. These are special trees and they only will listen to the I AM's followers." Amber Wind announced as they approached the cottage door. The whole thing looked like it would fall over just by looking at it besides it surviving this storm. Noticing Little Marie's concern when they landed on the tiny front porch, she added, "Don't judge a book by its cover my little one." Amber opened the door and entered.

"Ok but it sure looks like it's going to fall down." Little Marie entered looking back at Christina that was just behind her.

"There is a good reason this place looks like this and we will explain when we get inside." Christina closed the door behind them, and the room filled with a warm light. It was magnificent!

It was like a dream cottage with all the furniture and mirrors sparkling with crystal and silver and blue. "This is the snow Princess Abagail's cottage she uses when she visits the Island. She is from far north and is a great follower of I AM the Son Jesus. She has made this place of rest available for you. You need to remember where it is on the island!" Christina informed Little Marie before they sat down for the refreshments waiting for them on the table. This is when Christina tried to explain and prepare Little Marie for the storm that was coming for her and her family!

"The enemy is always wanting to steal and destroy the children of The I Am. In both your world's, here and there. We are here to help you in your fairy world dreams, to show you the love and power of The I AM to work out all things for good for those that love Him. When you put your hope and trust in I Am the Son the Christ, His Spirit will work in you and with you, to do great and mighty things. There is a time coming soon where you will need to lean on all you have learned from Them. They are your strength; your enemy has already been overcome but you have to walk that truth out in your own life. That is what is called –Carrying your cross, under grace! Amen." Christina ended as if she was praying and Amber Wind agreed, "Amen!"

Before Little Marie could ask any more questions, she was being awaken to her sister saying *"Wake up wake up! Come on Little Marie it's time to go on our picnic."* Christy was starting to pull her arm to wake her up. *"We are all waiting for you."*

"OK, OK I'm awake!" Little Marie said a bit too loudly. "Man, I just needed a few more minutes" She confessed more gently.

"Why? We have a great day ahead of us! Why would you want to sleep is beyond me? Come on." Christy rushed to the door with one more look back to make sure he sleepy sister was getting up!

Little Marie grabbed her backpack throwing in her favorite blanket and sneakers, not forgetting to be careful with her necklace she tucked it in the side pocket. Then she ran downstairs with something other than excitement. Was it worry? No, it was a foreboding! "Now I need to remember to trust Them." She whispered out loud.

~~~

"SMITHY come in?" Why is he not answering his walkie talkie! "Come in Smithy!" Burt yelled into his satellite walkie talkie wanting to throw it against the wall. He had been trying for the last half hour to get a hold of him. Now Smithy better be in a ditch somewhere dying or he was thinking about putting him in one!

"Come in Burt. Sorry I've been detained buddy, I had a little trouble with one of our guests. Everything's tied up and ok now," Smithy replied to the last communication sent. He was smiling and lighting a cigar looking down into the tear streaked face of #19. She was a pretty little thing that needed to be kept in control and he was just the one to do it.

Number 19 just closed her eyes vowing to herself to get away no matter what! She would just have to be watchful and patient for the right opportunity. She was not going to let these creeps take her anywhere else. She has learned fear is not an option, she must be strong if she was going to get away and survive.

"What the hell Smithy, where are you? We need to meet at the cave now!" Burt tried to calm down, thinking He would be rid of the idiot soon, he just needed to wait until the job was done. Then bye, bye, Smithy and hello money and no worries again! That thought made him get control. "Smithy see ya soon!"

"Roger that, I'm already here so see ya when you get here. Over and out." Then Smithy picked the girl up by the hair and said you better keep your mouth shut or you will get worse than I just gave you!" Then he tossed her into the corner of the damp cave, he paced back and forth hoping Burt will not notice the girl had been touched, but if he does, he had a story to tell anyway! He then walked out of the entrance of the back cave that led to a tunnel that led to several other small caves then to the entrance which to walk through you had to be small like a child, so he had to bend down to exit the damp dark place. Still smoking his cigar, he started to pace in front of the entrance humming to himself feeling a little cocky after his time with #19.

"Hey there idiot. I could smell that cigar a mile away. Do you want everyone to know we are here!" Burt quietly but firmly stated as he grabbed the cigar and put it out under his boot.

"Don't do that, those are expensive. No one is out this far in the woods to smell that anyway…" but before Smithy could say another word Burt smacked him up beside the head and pushed past him bending down to enter the cave.

"Why I ought a…" was all Smithy could say to the much taller, larger and not to add, smarter man that just happened to be his partner for now, he thought. He stooped down and followed Burt. When he caught up to him his heart sunk. Burt was standing in the doorway of number 19 frowning. This was not a place to get into a fight with a big man or was it?

Little Marie Grows Up

"What's the meaning of this?" He shouted at Smithy pointing to the blood on the girls lip that was starting to swell. Keeping calm, he walked in and untied the girl, while he gave her a small cloth to wipe the blood away herself. Then standing in the doorway he turned to confront Smithy.

Smithy was just leaning against the cave wall lighting another cigar.

"I thought I told you not to be smoking..." Burt started to say but Smithy cut him off by blowing out the match toward his face.

"No one is going to smell this from in here. And don't start in on me with that one. She has been a pain in the ass since we got her! I just needed to let her know who's in charge!" Smithy smiled and wink, but Burt was not amused.

Grabbing Smithy by the collar and bringing him face to face with him he shouted, "Well that certainly is not you! You were told not to lay a hand or anything else on any of the girls. They need to be untouched and pure looking as possible. I'm in charge when the boss is away and if I find you touching or hurting any of them, you will not be able to touch or hurt anyone again! Is that understood Mister!" Burt then through him down to the ground but being such a small place Smithy bounced against the far wall and almost back into Burt again. Burt was to fast as he backed into the small cave and Smithy landed on the floor at his feet. Bruised and humiliated he got up and glared for a moment into number 19's eyes and stalked past Bruce holding his cursing for the walk out into the open.

"I'm sorry I will not let him hurt any of you. Just behave and you will have a chance with your looks to get a wealthy master instead of some of the other things that will make the boss money. It's up to you where you end up. If your smart you will use your talents to get what you want." He then tired her hands again and telling her to stay he left her and the others in the dark.

By the time Burt got to the entrance where Smithy was waiting, he had reminded himself that he needed Smithy to finish this job and get number 20 and get off this Island.

"Hey there Smithy, I apologize for losing it back there but I'm responsible for the cargo being in prime condition! I do mean it hands off." He said less stern "but I didn't need to be so harsh!" Then Burt smiled and patted Smithy on the back as if they were old buddies. "Hey, I have a plan for number 20, so listen as we walk back and by tomorrow night, we will be cruising home with a fortune!"

The two men walked back talking softly about the plan that would change lives and futures.

Mommy called out "Hey girls make sure you put on your sun screen. I can help if you want." as they ran down to the beach ahead of the adults.

"We will." Christy called back as they reached the beach.

It was a beautiful warm sunny afternoon and the happy group enjoyed all the fun a picnic at the beach could bring. The water was just cool enough to scream when your bathing suit gets wet but then warms up as you get used to it. After a swim, then lunch the girls laid out on the beach to rest before going exploring later. Paul and Mommy told them the boundaries and they had to promise to stay together. Paul thought his little cove was a very safe place if the girls kept on the paths and around the property. No people or wild animals to speak of unless you hiked into the forest which was one of the boundaries. So, the happy group spent a beautiful day at the cove until around 3pm when the girls put there cover ups on and packed their backpacks with some treats and juice boxes from the picnic while pretending, they were going on a long adventure they kissed Mommy and Paul good bye, then waving dramatically for fun, as they ran down the beachy cove then up the path by the boat house.

"Paul it is safe for them to wonder around the grounds by themselves, isn't it?' Mommy asked as she bent her head to watch them as they went out of sight.

"Oh yes my dear no one is around except the grounds keeper and George and Martha. There are fences in the forest to keep most animals out, if the girls stay within the boundaries and not go in the forest or off the path around the cabins, they are very safe. They will obey the rules, won't they?" He then asked remembering he did not know the girls enough to answer that question himself.

"Yes, they are very good girls. Okay then if they are having their adventure time maybe we can have some time by ourselves too." Mommy smiled and then winked.

Paul jumped up and bowed before her. Then taking her hand "May I have this dance?"

She laughed as he pulled her to her feet and into his arms. Then spinning he started to Wallace on the sand. She melted into his arms and they danced the hour away until the time the girls were supposed to be back.

Taken

"Now remember we will have to do this fast and quiet. The ship leaves tonight and if everything goes in our favor, we will be out of here before any cops can be here to investigate the missing girls!" Burt whispered to Smithy as he watched the two girls walk past the boat house.

"Roger that!" Smithy said a little too loud.

"Did you hear that?" Little Marie asked thinking she hear a man's voice.

"Oh, that's probably the gardener I saw him early walking over here by the pool house." Christy pointed to the path they were just passing that led to the pool house. They had a place in mind to explore so they kept walking.

"Isn't this the best day ever?" Little Marie asked her sister. "I'm so happy you are my sister, you know."

"Yes, I know, but sometimes you can be a pain!" Christy laughed then pinched her little sister in the arm and ran up the path past her.

"Ouch, that hurt. Wait for me." She called as Christy turned the corner towards the forest. "Wait, where are you going? We aren't supposed to go near the forest…" Little Marie yelled as she turned the corner herself and saw no sign of Christy. "Where are you Christy, don't do this, you are scaring me!" As she said that a hand came around her mouth from behind and she tried to scream but to no avail. The hand was so tight that she passed out trying to breath. When she went limp her abductor threw her over his shoulder and ran into the forest without leaving a trace, or so he thought.

When she woke up, she was in a small cave, wet and cold. Shivering she sat up trying to see something in the blackness that surrounded her. Then see heard voices and they became louder as a faint light filled the room. "You better hope you didn't kill her?" Burt said to Smithy as he walked in the room with his flash light.

Little Marie shrunk down to the floor to lay in the position she remembered being when she woke up. She had an idea. Maybe if she acted like she was hurt or dead maybe they would leave her alone. Saying a silent prayer for help she relaxed as much as she could, to pretend she was dead.

"I didn't mean to make her stop breathing but she tried to scream, and we were too close to the beach that they might have heard her! So, what! We only needed the older one." Smithy said as Burt went over to look over Little Marie. She was limp and cold. He tried to hear or feel a heartbeat, but he felt nothing but his own heart beat pounding with frustration. So just after a minute he stood up and declared with amazing self-control, "You are right Smithy for once. Too bad for her but we can just leave her body here and take the twenty others. Let's get out of here!" Burt looked one more time at the little girl that was lying there dead, with a second thought he placed a blanket over her body. He walked out telling himself not to think about her again but knew that would now be impossible. He went to help Smithy to collect the others and get as far away as possible from this place. He promised himself, Smithy won't harm anyone again!

Finding the right time to take care of this guy, was going to be a priority.

"Smithy, line them up and tie them together." Speaking in a gentler voice he said to the captives "Ladies don't worry all will be fine. You will be taken care of as long as you behave. Now here I have some water for you all to drink before we leave. We will be going on a wonderful trip." Burt then handed each girl a small cup and filled it with water from a jug.

Number 19 was at the end with the new girl number 20 tied in front of her. She was so happy but also not to happy, to see her friend Christy from school. Misty said quietly without notice "Christy! It's Misty, how did you get here?"

Christy was still dazed from the shock of being abducted off the path by a tall large man but hearing her friends voice broke through the darkness she exclaimed "Misty it's you!"

"Who was that?" Burt looked down the line of twenty girls and saw the new girl crying on the shoulder of number 19. Thinking it was because she was new and having some light to see now was reacting, well this water will help that. He continued down the line number 10, 11," Here have drink sweetie."

After a minute, Misty whispered, "Shush down, yes it's me. You found me. But why are you here in the same awful situation, like me. Never mind, this is not the time for questions. Now listen to me don't drink that water! No matter what. Spit it out but don't drink it!"

"Why?" Christy whispered back, trying not to be noticed.

"Just trust me don't drink it! I have a plan. OK?" She spoke even softer because Burt was closer. Number 16, 17.

Christy said yes with her eyes and when Burt came to her she kept the water in her mouth until he moved on and then dribbled it out into her hands then to the ground, when he passed, so not to be noticed. Misty held it until they started walking and spit it out at the entrance. Once out in the open, the girls finally breathing fresh air for the first time for some in days, and whatever was in the water, made them all relax and giggle. Even Christy and Misty felt calmer but did not giggle.

"Come on girls follow me to the beautiful boat that will take you to your dreams." Smithy announced while Burt was smiling seeing the effects of the drug taking effect on the girls. He was becoming very confident that they were going to pull this off. And it was the last time he would ever get involved with sex trafficking. It got to him in a way he had not expected but thought he could handle this because of the money. Well Smithy made sure that would be hard to do but he thought his revenge would help the small conscience he had. Turning to the task at hand he grabbed the rope of the first girl and started guiding all of them away from the terrible cave. Burt moved up the line to lead and had Smithy go to the back. That's when Smithy started, pushing and poking at Misty.

"I'll get you, you old fart!" She thought. Looking ahead for any opportunity to get away.

◦∾◦

After Little Marie could not hear any voices anymore, she got up and slowly started to feel around hoping to find her backpack. The walls of the cave were cold and wet. In the dark her imagination wanted to take *off with fear as its guide. Ohhh no, her mind was starting to imagine, what would be awful to find in this damp black place! Oh please, not rats or maybe even big spiders. What was that she just stepped on? She froze in fear thinking the worst, but then she remembered something that calmed her, "This is like the cave in my fairy world and Jesus showed up and freed me! So now I know He is here, and I must be brave and strong to do what He has prepared me to do. Immediately she relaxed and moved forward. This time when her foot hit something, she did not get scared but bent down to feel what it was and to her happy surprise it was her backpack! "Thank you, Jesus!" She whispered and felt around in the side pocket hoping to find her necklace. "Please, please be there! Yes, here you are but will you shine in this world? Instead of putting it around her neck she wrapped the chain in her hand, holding the pendant out in front of her. "Please shine your light to help me out of this dark cave!" As Little Marie said this the cross in the center stone glowed a beautiful blue light showing her the way to the entrance. There she could see daylight and put the necklace back in backpack that was now on her back. She did not have any problem walking out of the small entrance, but she did so, very cautiously because she could hear something in the forest moving away, to her left. Peeking out, around the edge she saw the last of the captives disappear into the wooded forest next to the rock face of cliffs. Well now what! Should she follow them or get help? Her young mind was trying really hard not to cry, this all was very overwhelming but something deep inside her spoke to her if she would only calm herself and listen! "I Am with you. Follow to see where they go but do not let yourself be seen." "Yes", she thought," then I will be able to show Mr. Paul and Mommy where they all are." So Little Marie took off into the wooded forest to her left being as quiet and cautious as she could be while catching up to them. It was still light out, but she knew it was time they should have been home and Mommy would be worried. "I have to find Christy first, then I will go home to Mommy and Paul."*

Little Marie caught up with the group as they stopped by a steam to rest because some of the girls were weak from the days in the caves and whatever Burt put in the water, he gave them made them really relaxed. As she watched them, she saw the last two girls were Christy and Misty. "OH BOY!" She said a bit too loudly. Smithy looked in her direction but as he walked by Misty, she stuck out her foot and tripped him. That gave Little Marie enough time to move away from where she made the noise but closer to her sister and friend. Smithy got up and raised his bulky hand to smack her, but Burt was there in time to push him back to the ground.

"What the hell Smithy what do you have against her? I told you not to touch her!" Burt said standing over him with his fist raised. He was getting really tired of this guy and was counting the minutes until he could get rid of him.

"She tripped me, man. She had it coming. I also thought, I heard something over there." Smithy admitted while pointing in the direction of the noise but staying on the ground until Burt moved back. "I went to investigate and the little whore tripped me! You wouldn't take that from her, would you?" Smithy slowly got up and backed away from his partner.

"She wouldn't have tripped me!" He looked past her and saw nothing but was getting anxious sitting out here with twenty girls tied up together and one idiot partner. "Let's get moving. And you come up here for now Smithy!" Burt moved up to the front making the girls stand to get ready to move again.

Smithy followed a short distance behind Burt, grumbling to himself. "I'll get him and that little bitch too!" When Burt glanced back, he just smiled and kept walking.

After they all started walking again, Little Marie made herself known to Misty. A surprised, Misty, smiled then gave a worried glance at Smithy. Little Marie nodded and held up some small scissors that she found in her backpack and got close enough to pass them to her, from behind, then back she ran into the forest to hide. Misty wasted no time to cut her bindings and then help Christy while still keeping an eye on the two men just turning a corner. That was there chance and before Christy could hand off the scissors to the next girl, Misty pulled her into the forest toward Little Marie that they found hiding behind a large rock. They ducked behind with her to catch their breath.

"What? Where did you come from, Little Marie? I was hoping they didn't get you too! now here you are. Oh, Mommy is going to be so upset!" Christy coughed out between breaths.

Misty wasn't waiting for a discussion to ensue so blurted out "We don't have time for this now Christy! We need to get out of here before they come looking for us. I'm as surprised as you to see both of you! Man am I glad you are here but let's talk later." She looked at both of them with her frantic eyes and swollen lip and they shook their heads yes, then started moving deeper into the forest. Once they were further away, they heard a terrible scream then a sobbing sound that died down with in a minute.

"What was that?" Christy said looking back.

"It was an awful sound. Sounded like someone died?" Misty Answered.

"Let's go this way it looks familiar!" Little Marie said and ran off toward the sound of a water fall.

"Wait how would you know where we are Little Marie ...Stop!" Christy called but then went silent not wanting to be heard. So, the two older girls followed the little girl that had saved them and seemed to know the way!

Little Marie was so excited now to be seeing the similar surrounding of her fairy world. It was different but still the same and with her imagination she could see where they were and needed to go. Yes, look there is the edge of the forest and the lake. Shimmering lake. When the other girls caught up too Little Marie, they were all staring at a beautiful lake and the sound of a waterfall in the far distance. The sun was still shining but very low, so they needed to keep moving.

"This is beautiful, but we need to find help and get out of here!" Misty started shaking as she talked. Her fear and exhaustion were catching up to her and Christy started crying. Again, it was the youngest who took control and told them to be calm and follow her. Little Marie was off running back into the forest looking for something Christy thought. So, they followed hoping Little Marie knew what she was doing.

A short time later they came to a clearing that was full of green grass and wild flowers. Little Marie kept going past the pretty meadow turning a little more into the dense forest again but before the girls could complain they came upon two odd growing trees that grew along the ground with branches growing straight up. That's when they saw Little Marie disappear behind the trees.

"Where are we going?" They both said as loud as they dared.

"I'm in here. Please come in. You will be amazed!" Little Marie giggled. It is real. The cottage that she had just seen this morning in her dream world was standing right here. It looked the same small broken down front porch and door. The girls came through the branches of the giant trees to see Little Marie disappear again this time into the small cottage that looked like it would fall down any minute.

"Don't go in there, it will fall down on top of you! Come out! Come out now!" Christy started to cry again.

"Don't judge a book by its cover, Christy its safe for us. Come in here before those men find us." Little Marie said hoping that would make them come into the small rickety looking cottage. It worked they both ran past her into the small room. What they saw amazed them for sure. They looked around in awe and then feel down on the big cushions on the floor that were place around a table with flowers in a small vase. There was a small stove heating up a tea kettle and a table set for four! They all sat there mesmerized by the tiny beautiful room

---

"What the hell is happening out there!" The Boss man called out from the rustic house on the edge of a cliff overlooking the northeast side of the island. The ocean was rough and turbulent way down below but there was a small cove that had steep stairs leading to it where a boat waited.

"Whoever found that Smithy for this job, is the one who has to answer to me! Where is he?" Burt burst through past The Boss-man, ready to tear the place down.

"Calm down, you brute! He is down at the boat waiting for you two and the cargo. Where is it?" The Boss came up to pat Burt on the shoulder and hand him a drink.

After gulping down the whiskey in the glass, he sat down to explain the disastrous day!

"You mean you killed him right in front of the girls? Oh you, really lost it this time buddy! What am I going to do with you?" The Boss-man downed his drink trying to think of what to do. "Ok where is the body?"

"I put it behind a stump and put lots of branches and stuff over it. It will be hard to fine. That's not the problem it's the two girls that got away and the little girl that that bastard killed. We left her body in the cave! I'm freaking out here Boss-man. That Smithy caused all this and that's why

Little Marie Grows Up

I want to have a chat with Casper!" Burt finish the last of his drink and went to pour some more in his glass, thinking it would calm him down.

"Don't worry buddy we will be out a here soon. If Smithy killed the little brat to bad. When they find the body and his body then they won't think of looking any further he got what he deserved. The other two are a problem because they can identify you, so you my friend will have to stay out of the states for a long time. But with the money you're getting, yours and now Smithy's, you don't ever have to come back here again!" The Boss-man then walked over to the window to see Casper taking the precious cargo one by one down to the boat. Only three to go. He was getting out of this business dealing with live cargo. It was not his thing but maybe one or two pretty ones would make it a better trip to market. He laughed to himself it was almost over. "Hey Buddy, get ready, we are almost home free!"

"Good, I've been ready yesterday!" Burt stormed out to help with the last "one" to get on board the boat.

"The Boss-man will meet us at the Ship later, let's go dude!' Casper said to Burt as he started the engine.

"Fine let's go! We will have time to talk on the way!" Burt pushed the last girl into the bottom of the boat locking the door behind her. Then he sat down to wait for the right time to have that chat with Casper

"It looks like it's brand new inside here! How did you know about this place Little Marie?" Christy asked still looking around at all the pretty things decorating the cottage. Inside it was twice as big as it looked outside, with pretty white lace curtains on the windows a small couch in front of the fireplace and cute tiny kitchen where the kettle starting "whistling" louder and louder, causing the girls to jump. All of suddenly a petite young lady came into the room to take the kettle off the stove.

"I hope you, young lady's, are hungry?" She said without looking at them. She just busily prepared a tray of little cakes and muffins with a bowl of fresh fruit. She placed the tray on the table and then with the tea kettle she poured a little into each cup. The girls were cowering in the corner wondering what to do. This person seemed to expect them but never has looked at them once. "There are three girls here in my cottage are there not?" The pretty little lady said turning around but not seeing.

"Yes miss, we are here. Were you expecting us?" Little Marie was the first to realize the lady was blind but even more remarkable she looked like her Fairy god Mother, Christina. Now this was getting stranger by the moment.

"Why yes, I had hoped you would find your way here, my dears. I'd heard you needed help. My name is Cindy. Here sit down and rest." Cindy point to the pillows and then she sat to serve herself. "Please help yourselves as I'm not able to serve you but I can help you." Sipping her tea and listening to the girls starting to sit around the table. She smiled and it lite up the room.

"Thank you so much, Cindy." They said in unison, then they grabbed some of the muffins and cake. They were hungry especially Misty. After a few bits and then sips of warm tea, Misty thought to ask, "How did you hear about us needing help?" She wiped a crumb from her mouth feeling so much stronger by just eating something.

"Well let's just say a little fox told me." Cindy giggled to herself. The girls smiled but only for a moment. Even though they were in a beautiful charming place, being taken care of, they did not forget the two men that could be looking for them right at this moment.

"This is very odd but familiar to me. You remind me of my ah…" Little Marie looked at Christy and Misty and decided to let them know about her fairy world because now that they both are some of the girls that had been taken and with this strange but welcome experience happening right now it seemed the perfect time to let them know about her dreams. "Ah my fairy god mother, Christina? I also have seen this place and met a Foxman in my dreams! Do you know anything about that Cindy?" Little Marie questioned her.

"Well in a way your dreams have been used to guide you for such a time as this. The Great I Am has prepared a path and ways to help you in this fallen world. I am here because He wanted me to be. Do you understand Little Marie?" And she smiled again and even the other girls were amazed at her beauty when she smiled. She glowed.

"Well I don't know about her, I don't understand any of this, but I don't care right now! I am thankful we found you and now we need a *phone or a car to get us out of here!"* Misty almost started to cry but would not let herself fearing if she let even on tear out, she would become hysterical. From her past she had learned how to hold things in and she was using every effort now to not fall apart.

"Yes, I understand you have been through so much Misty, but you are loved and cherished. You also Christy! Little Marie already knows this truth. But this is all over whelming so for the moment refresh yourselves and rest. I am very sorry, but I do not have a phone or a car. I have chosen to live my life away from people and live in the forest with its wonderful creatures. They don't have so much hate and negativity that the city life seems to bring about! My brother comes by with supplies and to check on me but otherwise no one knows I'm out here. My cottage is disguised to look like it is falling down to keep everyone away." Cindy hoped they would believe her, then got up and went to get a few blankets for the girls because she could not let them leave now that it is sunset, they will have to stay the night and then in the morning she would walk them out to the nearest neighbor about a mile away. After explaining this to the girls and assuring them that no one will find them here she tucked them in in front of the fire and left them rest.

Instead they talked about Little Marie's dreams. Christy was starting to put two and two together as Little Marie told her of her amazing adventures in her dream fairy world! She had noticed her little sister had seemed different ever since the other day she saw her having what she thought was a nightmare. Now hearing that she met an angel, a mermaid and fairies and ultimately Jesus who she calls the I Am Jesus the Son.

Now Misty liked the story but that was all it was to her. She had always felt a lone and unloved as long as she remembered. If she was loved and cherished then why did all these men hurt her and even her mother did nothing to stop it, so "No I don't believe it but it's a nice coincidence or fairytale." Misty announced after Little Marie finished her tale of the cottage dream just this morning. She then rolled over wanting to go to sleep.

"Misty that's understandable but I have seen a change in Little Marie and she sure has a lot of things that seemed to help her help us. We would not have found this place and we would be out in the cold night staving right now, so I'm going to give her some faith for now. Let's sleep now and first thing in the morning we will go home!" Christy kissed Little Marie on the forehead and thanked her.

"Thank you for all your help today, Little Marie. And yes, I would like to sleep now. Goodnight!" Misty said as she thought to herself, must be nice to be so innocent to believe in a fairy world. I can't believe in that stuff anymore after what I've been through in my life! This was her last thought before falling into a much needed, deep sleep.

"Good night you guys. I'm so glad to be able to help you, Thank God." She whispered then waiting until they both were asleep. She put her necklace on and was back in her fairyland but not in the cottage. Instead she was sitting on a log in a small cove. She heard a loud roar of a waterfall to her left. It was so beautiful here. She just sat there at first taking in the beauty and the way the midday sun shined through the trees to the sandy beach. A large cliff was to her right going straight up and she noticed nothing was growing on top of it. Across the cove was a forest lining the beach and a large cave entrance toward the point of land that jutted out to the ocean.

"Well this is a wondrous place. I have not been here before." She quietly spoke out loud wondering if any of her fairy friends might be here also.

"Hello Little Marie, I'm so glad you like it. It is one of my favorite places on this Island." Mercy the ocean fairy popped up out of the water spun around drying herself and flew over to sit by Little Marie.

"Oh Mercy, how are you? I have not seen you since the gathering." Little Marie said.

"I'm happy to see you, again, Little Marie" Mercy replied.

Little Marie explained, "I met your cousin Grace the lake fairy. She spoke very highly of you and now I remember why I wanted to talk with you. We think we have seen Sarah the Mermaid that is missing. She goes to swim at the lake, but no one has been able to talk with her as far as I know." Little Marie remembered things could be happening here while she was awake!

"Well this is a special place. It's called Mercy Cove. Do not worry Sarah the mermaid Queen is here. This is where anyone can take refuge from the enemy and his lies. See the cave over there?" Mercy pointed across the cove to the large cave opening and said "Only those seeking *truth and mercy can enter it and only the followers of I AM the Son can see the entrance to it. So those that receive the grace and mercy of the I AM the Father, on rescue point are guided to the entrance that is revealed to the seekers. Then they have a choice to receive the grace and walk into the cave to take the gift of truth, which is the protection from the enemy and brings a peace that is not of any world. It is free for those that believe in the I AM the Son of the Creator or they can reject the gift and go away continuing to wander. This choice leads them back out to sea. Some believing enough to want to please the I AM, by trying to live independently by His laws to show they can do it without Him. Everyone falls short of any of these laws, but Jesus the Son paid the complete and final price so now love, mercy and grace can be received and opened. If you receive it, you will be living in grace not condemnation of the law. It is the truth that sets you free to enjoy life and that is good news! Now some just don't believe they deserve forgiveness, and some don't believe in the I AM the Creator at all, so they go throughout time going up and down with the waves of life, believing what feels good or makes sense to them. Even believing in their own created things which become their Idols."* She sighed then added, *"It is a place of hope and choices. You must explore and remember as you have with your other adventures in this fairy world, it might be useful in your world."*

"That is wonderful to hear because I see the cave entrance and it's bigger than that cliff over there." Little Marie pointed to the looming cliff to their right. *"Well it seems as big."* She smiled.

"That is amazing. Because that is the cliff of Lies and if you see the cave of Refuge entrance as larger than the Lies, you truly are understanding to rest in Him who is perfect to bear your burdens and wants you to join Him with open arms. You see the Lies are small compared to the truth of Jesus and grace. That cliff is a big distraction to those who focus on self and believe truths that seem right, but Lies always has twisted, making partial truth that can become wicked. When they focus on the cliff and not the Cave entrance, they wander off discouraged because they see the Lies as truth and it becomes too big to climb. It brings to their minds all their fears, doubts and shame. The longer they focus on it, the more twisted their truth becomes and they don't see the cave of Refuge anymore. So, they go through rough seas again, alone." Mercy had a tear fall from her

eye talking about all those who took that path back out to sea. She had seen so many in her day but then looking up at Little Marie's sweet face she was reminded that many did chose grace and enter into God's refuge and loving arms. She then smiled and flew up and then down diving into the water again. "Good bye, Sweet Little Marie, I have enjoyed our time together." Then she was swimming out to the mouth of the cove, before going deeper she once more waved to her knew little friend and then was gone.

"Bye, Bye sweet Mercy!" Little Marie called out and decided to not waste any more time sitting there and started to go explore this wonderous place. Who knew when she would be woken up?

⁓

Back at the hidden cottage, deep in the woods, the hide out for the girls. Casper was wondering why he was still standing on the decrepit old porch. "Why are you not asking me inside, my dear?" he asked his sister with a smile she could not see.

"I'm wanting to clean up first, I was not expecting you this morning? Please have a seat in the backyard and I'll bring some coffee. It will only take me a few minutes my sweetheart. And Oh, if you brought any supplies just leave them on the porch. Thank you!" Cindy then closed the door almost in his face. She waited to hear him put something down and walk away toward the backyard. She then hurried over to where the girls were before, but they were not there. "Girls, where are you?" she whispered. All three had woken up to the sounds on the front porch so they, were hiding in the corner. "It's alright that was my brother, but I don't want to explain you girls to him, so I need you to hide in the closet in my room." At that statement she heard them scamper off without a question just a whispered "OK" as they passed her. She hurriedly fixed some hot water for the instant coffee she had for such an emergency.

Casper waited in the quaint back yard, thinking, "That was not unusual for my sister to act like that with other people but not me. I wonder what's up?" He had worried in the past of how stable she was to not like people so much she wanted to live on this island basically alone! But the past few months he saw her beauty come back when she smiled

Little Marie Grows Up

which was much more and more often. The climate and the peace here has worked wonders since the accident that blinded her but more than that scared her emotionally for life. He would just go with her moods and keep a close eye on her. Thankfully she is unaware of where he has been living or how he has been making a living. She still thinks the money from the settlement was still paying for her but that has been gone for more than a year. His life changed also that awful night. He was glad she did not know he was partially to blame for her losing her daughter and her eye sight. Every day since he renewed the vow he made that terrible day to always take care of her. His thoughts were interrupted by Cindy.

"Here you go sweetheart. How are you this morning?" She asked after handing him the cup and then finding a seat next to him.

"Why thank you my dear. I'm doing fine just wanted to stop by to bring you some supplies because I am going to be gone for a few days." He explained, then wanting to go inside "It's a little cold out here for you isn't it? Can we please go inside?" He asked with genuine concern.

"Oh, why yes we can, but I find it very refreshing in the morning air. I can still picture in my mind the way the dew drops looked on a rose petal in the first morning light. Now it's the fresh feel of the air and the sounds of the forest animals, that I enjoy most." She said with a small smile crossing her lips.

He helped her up and held her arm to walk her into the cottage. "You know I can get around here just fine without you, but I would not want to have too! Where are you going and when will you be back?" She inquired.

"Well, it's sort of a sailing trip to drop some cargo off and then I will be back before you know it." He said thinking ... Only long enough to pick her up and take her to their new life on an island where he would never be found! Then he added "I have brought enough food for a week, but I will not be that long. I also brought the supplies you requested last week. So, will you be OK? I'll tell Mr. Paul and he will check on you if you would like?"

"I will be fine, and I am glad you found some work. Be safe and I will not need to be checked on except by you!" Her voice raised a little with her last statement. She kissed him on the forehead and walked him to the door. "I love you and thank you for everything.

His heart sank, please don't thank me! If you only knew, no she can never know. "Ok but I am letting him know for an emergency only! I will call him if I need to get you a message. I will leave my walkie-talkie with him that way you don't have to worry about him coming up here. Make sure yours is charged. I've got to get going or I'll miss my boat. Goodbye my dearest sister and keep yourself safe." He kissed her forehead and they hugged.

"You take care of yourself and come back soon, Love you!" Cindy closed the door as he was saying "I love you too!"

After a few minutes passed she called to the girls and they came out from hiding to ask, "who was that?"

"That was my brother, but I did not want to have to explain you three to him, so I had you hide. He is a wonderful man and you do not have to be afraid of him. Now are you hungry?" Cindy asked while going into the kitchen then remembering the supplies on the porch, she asked the girls, "will you please bring in the boxes of supplies in from the porch and I will make breakfast."

"Sure, we are hungry but after that we must get going!" Christy said knowing Mommy would be worried sick. Misty and Little Marie brought in the two boxes that were on the porch and they all sat down to eggs and bacon with hot coco to drink.

"Thank you so much Cindy. This is so nice of you to help us like this." Misty said. "Let us help clean up for you before we leave."

"It is my pleasure to help you and thank you. Now I think I will go with you girls to make sure you make it home. Let me get dressed for the trip. I'll be right back." She was actually finding herself excited to go out but it was only because of these girls she told herself. The girls cleaned up the cottage and themselves the best they could while they waited to go home.

Of course, after a long night waiting and now its morning with no information, Mommy was ready to go search for her girls at first light.

Martha had insisted she eat something and wait a little longer because there was no one to go with her.

"Okay Martha but I will be going out right after breakfast! No one is going to stop me from finding out what is going on and where my girls are." Mommy said and sat down waiting for her breakfast. Martha went back to the kitchen trying to stall, thinking that's what Mr. Paul would want her to do.

But nothing was going to stop her! She burst into the kitchen, grabbed a bagel and juice box. Without another word, she walked calmly out the back door of the kitchen. No one will tell her what to do when it comes to her family! Mommy took a bite of the fresh bagel and turned the corner of the house to walk past the entrance toward the path that the girls had taken the afternoon before. "Oh, please be alright!" she was saying when all of the sudden the girls, came running up to her with Misty and a young woman, following right behind them! She dropped everything and ran up to them, then falling to her knees she hugged her children. The girls hugged her back saying, "Mommy we are home! Look we found Misty!"

"Oh my God you are safe and yes home! Misty oh my how did that happen? Here let's get you inside and cleaned up. We can talk all about it." Mommy said while herding the girls inside, not noticing the young lady that starting walking back toward the path using her walking stick, until Little Marie called out, "No don't go Cindy, you must come in and meet Mommy!" Little Marie ran out to her and throwing her arms around the lovely little woman, begging her to come into the house. Realizing Little Marie was not going to let go until she agreed, Cindy whispered "Ok, but only for a moment." She turned around with Little Marie holding her hand she walked up the steps into the house while Mommy was busy looking over Christy and Misty to assure herself they were genuinely alright. Then she looked up and said, "Whom might this lovely young lady be?"

Misty answered before anyone else. "This is Cindy and she let us stay in her cottage last night and brought us here this morning! She is like our guardian angel. Little Marie found her strange cottage out in the forest." She was so very happy to be safe and was enchanted by Cindy.

"Oh, my goodness, Thank You so very much, Cindy! You must come in! Oh my, here let me help you." Mommy was surprised to see Cindy was blind. She was so natural walking with her walking stick, that Mommy just had not noticed. "Here let's sit over here on the couch and I'll have Martha bring some refreshments."

But the girls all wanted to clean up, so she allowed them to go upstairs.

After a while, Mommy came up to the circle of girls that were sitting on the floor looking out at the cove and asked, "How are you girls? Do you think you are able to answer some of the Sheriff's questions? I will be right there, and Cindy decided to stay for a while also."

They looked at each other, then holding each other's hands and getting up, they nodded yes. They walked past Mommy downstairs and sat down on the couch across from the now blazing fire in the fire place.

After the questioning of Misty and the girls the Sheriff replied, "Oh my, Misty that is a terrible thing to go through young lady. Do you think you could describe the men that abducted you?" Misty shook her head yes. Then he asked, "Now Christy, can you tell me what happened to you?" After he received the same information from Christy and Little Marie, he concluded he needed to call the FBI and coast guard before he did anything else. There were still 18 girls on a boat getting away.

The door of the cabin burst open and Mr. Paul came running into the house calling out "Girls, girls are you alright?" Mommy was the first to meet him and hugged him telling him everything was alright. A little calmer he rushed up to them and picked them up into his arms and hugged them. "I was so worried about you two. Oh, Three?" He looked around with confusion seeing Misty there also, then laughed out loud "Thank God you are all alright!" Mr. Paul set them down and they all had time to talk and catch him up on what the girls had explained.

"I will have to get the coast guard and the FBI involved seeing this is kidnapping and seems maybe human trafficking of these girls. If they think they can use my island, they better think again!" The Sheriff explained to Mommy and Paul after sending the girls up to their bedroom. "There are still girls on a ship out there as we speak, and we need to set up a rescue before they get into international waters. I will be back in soon. They will probably want to set up some kind of base to coordinate the rescue, this might be a good place to do that if that is Okay, Paul?"

"Why yes, they can use the empty cabin on the property next door to George and Martha's cabin. An old friend uses it when he visits but he has not been here for over a year or so. Just let me know when they get here and it will be ready." Paul replied then he excused himself to get cleaned up from being in the forest all night.

Back at the ship Burt was planning his next move. "Hey Casper when you have a moment, I need you back here." Burt yelled up to where his small shipmate was walking. This would be tricky now that the captain and crew were aboard. He still wanted to have a chat about that Smithy character, and he wasn't going to wait any longer. Besides he could keep his cool when he needed too.

"So, you wanted to see me?" Casper came around the corner toward the back of the ship where Burt was playing with a rope.

"Yes, I did. I want to know where in the hell you met Smithy? Who does he hang with and who is his family?" Burt started to tie the rope into knots while he questioned Casper. His face tight with anger.

"Whoa man, don't know what you're talking about. Smithy was not a friend of mine! He is a sleaze ball if you ask me. I just met him in SE Portland at a seedy bar off of 82nd. The boss wanted someone that was needing money and had no one to go home too. I hung out a few days to check him out and told the boss about him. That's all man, I don't know him personal like." Casper kept his distance but tried to look causal not wanting to push Burt over the thin edge he was clearly walking. "What happened, man? He do something stupid or something?"

"You could say that." Was all Burt was going say, this time around. "Casper you better be telling me the truth or you won't like the consequences." After giving him his famous "don't mess with me" glare, he walked away without letting Casper answer.

That's fine, Casper thought, he didn't need him to be his friend, but he didn't want him as an enemy either. This was going to be an interesting voyage and for some their last, he thought to himself. Gulping down the guilt that was trying to choke him at every turn. He was getting good at pushing it way down these last few years having to help his dear sister. He had to make up for the accident before he could ever move on with his own life. Now he found himself doing desperate, despicable things to pay for the surgeries that would give his sister back her sight but if she knew how he got the money she would never forgive him, let alone use it for herself. Yes, guilt was becoming his regular companion with shame standing in line to accuse him whenever he could quiet the battles of guilt in his mind. "Well Casper you've done it again, jumped into it deep this time. You need to finish what you started and then be out for good!" he said quietly to himself walking back into the main cabin area. There was a big storm coming and they needed to batten down the hatches.

༺❀༻

"My darlings, I am so glad you are alright." Mommy hugged her girls again when they were alone. "What would you like to do today? I think it should be a restful day and we will need to talk some more about everything but when you girls are ready." Mommy wanted to make sure they were alright emotionally, too.

"Mommy, it's ok. We really are alright. I am sort of worried about Misty, though. What is going to happen to her when we go home? She does not want to go back to that awful place with her Mom, you know why." Christy felt fine but wanted her friend to be Okay too. Misty had been through so much more than Christy ever had. Christy thought trying not to think of the bad man babysitter. "Can she live with us?"

"You are such a sweetheart, Christy. This is very complicated, and the adults will have to work this out for her but we will try to think of a good solution for all concerned. For today though Misty said she wanted to walk Cindy back to her cottage and Cindy was over joyed to have the company. They left a while ago but will be back when the FBI people get here. Maybe you two would show me the way to Cindy's cottage and we can pick them up." Mommy's answer was good enough for now.

Little Marie sat in her Mommies lap and prayed for a happy ending for Misty and all of them while she listened instead of talking, for once. She realized she was having more self-control and how good it felt to listen. She then could pray Jesus would work it out. This was way too big for her to figure out but that was okay, because she knew God was way big enough! There was a calmness and peace inside her to just happily sit with her family feeling the love and protection of her creator.

Little Marie Grows Up

"Well now, you have been awfully quiet, Little Marie. Are you alright?" Mommy brushed the few hairs hanging out of place on her littlest girl's sweet face. She suddenly was having a hard time not thinking of her baby left for dead in a dark cave. She was so very proud of her girls, to be so strong and brave. Something was different about her youngest, but she couldn't put her finger on it? It must be Little Marie was growing up faster than she thought.

"I'm fine. Just happy to be home right now. I can show you Cindy cottage when you need me too." Little Marie smiled at Christy. Christy winked and said with a giggle, "Yes Mommy Little Marie knows the way."

This was very strange for both her girls to be so calm and collected, even giggling after such an ordeal. Well, she shouldn't complain they were her remarkable children. Maybe something else was happening here? Seems there has been some kind of divine intervention, but too many questions still needed to be answered here. Mommy's thoughts continued to recount the past few days and even weeks as she tried to understand all that had happened. She shivered thinking of the things that could have happened to her girls. Then she remembered all the other girls still out there. "So how many girls do you think are still needing to be found?" She asked all of the sudden.

"I'm not sure but I think at least 15 girls. Misty probably knows for sure. I hope the Sheriff finds them!"

Christy replied sadly. Worry started creeping into her mind.

"I prayed for them so I'm sure they will be rescued!" Little Marie said with a hopeful smile.

"You girls stay here while I go talk to the grownups and find out when the FBI will be here." Mommy kissed her girls on their foreheads and left them in the beautiful bedroom.

Christy turned to her sister and asked, "How do you know they will be rescued?"

"Well, I prayed. And this is kind of like the first time I met Jesus in my fairy world, when he gave me the necklace. The island we are on is a lot like the Island in my dreams. Christina and I rescued 20 girls from caves that remind me of the caves, the guys had taken us!" She laughed out loud. "I'm a little girl that The Great I Am God has a plan for me to help others through my dreams. Showing me His power and that His love and truth conquers all the enemy's lies and attacks. I hope someday you can know Jesus, too!" Little Marie smiled up at her sister and saw the sadness and confusion in Christy's beautiful brown eyes.

"That is a really good story, but I think you are just lucky or something! Anyways, I hope we can stop talking about this and talk about something different." Christy said feeling almost anger that her sister could be so sure and happy about such things when so many things were still so bad! Chaulk it up to, Little Marie's imagination and her being so young. I have experiences and can remember a lot more disappointment and pain in my life than Little Marie could ever know! She thought to herself almost wanting to cry but holding back because she was the oldest and had too!

Little Marie waited a minute and then hugged her sister whispering "I know you are scared and feel alone but we are loved and not alone. You will see." Then she just sat there resting quietly until Christy dozed off from her tears. This time it felt good for Christy to let go and not be the strong one. This was a first of many times to come where the oldest leans on the youngest. With a smile on her sweet face and a peace in her heart, Little Marie ran off to her bed to put on her special necklace and again was instantly back in her fairyland, but something was wrong!

It was very dark and stormy. She was flying above the Cliffs of Lies, looking down into Mercy Cove. She could see out to the ocean. There was a huge wall of dark thunderous clouds heading right for the Island and the cove. It was like a black wave rolling in the sky just over the big gray waves of the ocean. Her heart skipped a beat looking down the sharp steep cliffs to the bottom where there was a boat coming into the cove.

"Is anyone here with me?" Little Marie called out.

"Of course, sweetheart, remember you are never alone!" Christina flew up beside her.

"Oh, that's funny, I just told my sister that same thing and I truly believed it! But when I came here and saw the storm and looked down the cliffs, I became afraid again and forgot that Jesus The I AM is always with me." Little Marie said with a laugh.

"And He sent me to remind you of that exact thing. I am here to help in any way you may need!" Christina bowed in midair and smiled her lovely smile. "There are a lot of things a foot and we need to be careful not to be seen. That is why you were sent up here. To see the "big picture"! But when looking down the Cliff of Lies one must take care to remember the truth of the Love of the Great I Am Jesus or one can start believing lies that come into one's head! You see that over there at the point at the entrance of Mercy cove. It's there as a reminder of His mercy and it is a beacon of hope and refuge for the lost. Look up and ahead before looking down and behind!" Christine pointed ahead to the right as she spoke.

"Yes, I see it! It's a large wooden cross with beautiful flowers growing on the ground all around it. Oh, it is so beautiful but what's it doing up there? I couldn't see it from the beach down in the cove?" Little Marie flew a little closer to look down at the cove again. Yes, the boat was there and what looked like Brutal and his companions. They were unpacking something by the entrance to Refuge Cave and then Brutal started walking over to the bottom of the cliffs. Before he looked up Little Marie and Christina flew back over the top of the cliff and then down the right side into the old growth forest.

"We can follow the Misty River to Rescue Point. There we can see what is going on without being seen." Christina said while leading the way.

It sure was wonderful being a fairy being able to fly, making it easy to hide while seeing things far above. As they flew along the river, just above the water, Little Marie was amazed at the sparkling beauty all around the river's edge. It was all refreshed by the water from the river that was always flowing, bringing life to all that lived there. Even the rocks seemed to cry out," Isn't the Creator amazing." They were covered in soft green moss where the tiny Sprit's, tiny cousins of the woodland fairy's, made their homes in the crevices not easily seen except the tiny puffs of smoke coming up between the moss and rocks. Then as if their presence flying by had triggered something, the creatures and the tiny Sprits along the river edge became busy fliting and scurrying around like they were preparing for something. Maybe the storm! There was no time to find out when Christina stopped for a second at the fork in the river and said, "We need to turn left here to get to the bottom of the cross at Refuge Point. Please follow closely because I will show you a secret entrance to Refuge Cave!" Christina said with a smile, she turned and Little Marie followed very close indeed.

<hr>

At the ship just off the Orcas Island coast, The Captain told the crew, over the intercom. "This storm is going to be a doozy! We are going to go around the other way to wait it out before going out to sea." "It's a fast-moving, spring storm so we will make a break for it once it passes. Stand by for further orders. Over and Out!" Captain Raymond was not going to take any chances with this ship or cargo. It was the last time he was going to do this type of voyage! He grumbled to himself. Little did he know he was right!

Burt burst into the cabin "Oh no we are not going to hang back until the storms blows over! There are too many lose ends on that Island we just left behind. There is going to be way too much heat coming our way to just sit anywhere around these Islands, the Boss is not going to happy about this!" He slammed his fist on the console making his point.

"Whoa, whoa calm down man. That's not my fault you left a trail for them to follow. I'm captain of this ship and I make all the decisions for this voyage. The boss is very clear on that! You just go relax, I have a few back up plans for just such an occasion." Captain Raymond open the cabin door to invite Burt to leave. He was a tall man but lean so compared to Burt he felt small, but he was the Captain of the ship, so with a commanding authority, he asked Burt to go and "wait below with the cargo!" Burt just pushed past him making sure his size was intimidating but said nothing more. The Captain went back to guiding the ship to the plan B area. As the fog and clouds started to roll in, he carefully navigated his ship close to the front entrance to the deep cove where he had a small boat waiting. They would get the "live" cargo to safe cover until the storm past. With that idiot leaving a trail a mile long the authorities were bound to know to be looking for a ship and he thought if he was boarded by the authorities, they would find only grain and wine as their cargo. No one knows about the places in the cove that were perfect to hide anything or *one you needed too. He smiled feeling very proud of himself. Just a few days and they would be in international waters and home free!*

In Little Marie's fairy world, Christina wanted to show Little Marie what would help her be a hero. "Here we are! Now don't be afraid just trust me and follow close. You have been prepared for such a time as this!" Christina winked, then before Little Marie could question her, she flew over the edge of the cliff of Refuge Point, down the windy steep slope and into the side of the rock wall of the cliff! Thankfully Little Marie didn't hesitate and followed Christina into what looked like a wall with no way in! As she blindly followed, the currents of the wind changed helping them fly perfectly without effort and just at the perfect time, as they would seem to be hitting the rock wall, an opening appeared just big enough for them to enter.

"Oh my, that was exciting." Christina laughed while resting against the cool rock wall of the cave. "You're so brave Little Marie! See what faith does. It changes what seems to be impossible into possible. For The Creator nothing is impossible. Faith in Him and His son Jesus brings what believer's call miracles and non- believer's think of as magic or coincidence. Yet God, I Am whom I am, The Creator of the universe is wanting to work through His creation to show His love, mercy and grace. His ways are not our ways." Christina paused to see if Little Marie was still listening. Seeing that she was with a smile she continued. "Little Marie the truth of the victory The I Am has taken when He allowed His beloved Son to be born and then die to unite mankind back to Himself is a picture of true love The Creator has for mankind. His power showed when Jesus the Son became alive again has change everything for mankind. It's a hard one to figure out if you are using adult human reasoning but as a child you can have the strongest faith and imagination to become what The Father created you to be. It is written on your hearts you know, that's why the enemy attacks all human children through any means he can with Lies and Fear. Stealing their innocence and hope. If that does not work, he will use Pain and Suffering, but with God Pain and Suffering will be used for good in the long run. All will understand in the end of this age but for now faith is the only way."

Little Marie was amazed again, which was becoming a normal occurrence in her dreams! It seemed the beauty and peace that came with the excitement of faith was becoming a part of her now. She was able to believe because she was a child so maybe that's why she was experiencing a miracle in this fairy world of dreams. Yet she was also able to understand and believe what she heard in this dreamworld, much better than when she was an awake eight-year-old little girl. "I think I'm starting to understand after all these dreams The I AM, God loves us! Meeting Jesus has helped me know that. Faith in Them both is what saved me and now I have the power to stand up against the enemy because of The Holy Spirit They gave me? Is that right? Wow this is so wonderful to understand! Thank you, thank you for helping me know these things." Little Marie almost shouted while she spun around with her excitement but quickly remembered to be quiet.

"Little Marie when you listen and hear take time to know it's the Word of God or not. The Holy Spirit, which you do have my sweet, will help you understand the truth and you will succeed. The thing to watch out for is Fear and Lies because they can lead you down a long deep dark path. If they are believed and followed, they will steal the hope and good purpose of the ones believing them., The Father planed for them. God is working with mankind's knowledge of good and evil, also with man's free will to choose good or evil. Well so is the enemy… Oh look…" Christina lowered her voice to a slight whisper, "Down there, something is going on. We better check to see since we are here. The Great I AM who I AM may have a purpose for such a time as this." Christina pointed to a perfect ledge to spy on the scene unfolding below at the bottom of a large cave. They quietly flew over to a ledge and peered down on a gathering, of the Enemies followers!

Lies was speaking loudly, while flitting back and forth, trying to talk over Fear. "You always get more attention, don't you?! Well without me, no one would believe you because your power comes from them believing me!" Lies stopped in front of Fear with a smile of victory on his pointy little face.

"Yes, yes Lies, we have all heard it before yet I'm the reason they keep believing you so like it or not, we are a productive team. Our master is very happy with our work, plus I am the one who makes things very interesting you know." Fear proudly flew away to show what He loved to do.

Little Marie looked to where he was headed and saw several girls sitting on the sandy floor of the cave leaning against the cold wall. All of a sudden one of the smallest girls screamed and fainted as Fear flew past her ear. Then another girl screamed while trying to get away from something not there. The next girl screamed and fainted like the first. She watched as Fear flew through the cave and saw the joy he got from every scream. Then he stopped and flew back up to the spot where the group was gathered. "Ta dumb!" Boasting he bowed, "You see, Lies, how fun and easy that was!" He said smiling from pointy ear to pointy ear.

Pride could not keep quiet any longer! This two always got on his nerves. "You know, Fear, we all have our ways to make the Master happy so why don't you just shut up for once." Pride interrupted Fears boasting having heard enough. He knew he was very powerful because after all Pride is why the Master is who he is! "So stop goofing off! You have things to do hear. Get to it, meet back at the chosen place." He said with a voice filled with authority. He may look more dignified than the others, but his wings were small and tattered just like all the other fallen ones.

"I guess that's what Pride does best. Looking like something he is not!" Little Marie thought as she watched him fly off with the group leaving Lies and Fear lurking down on the human group in the cave.

Gun Shoots by the Lake – The Plan

Little Beth smiled at that comment. "I love this story Miss Marie. I like Little Marie, she is smart. Keep going!" She encouraged me to go on.

"Yes Marie, I want to hear more too. You never told this story before? I want to know what happens!" Jenny said with a genuine smile.

"I am a little amazed at the story myself. Most is true from memory, but some things are new to me and I am enjoying telling it. I'm so glad to tell it." I said beginning again but before I could Buddy jumped up and started baying and barking scaring all of us, then several gun shots were fired in the direction Manchester went.

"Quiet Buddy, Come here." I said while grabbing the leash. "Jenny please take Beth in the bedroom and lock the door. We will be back in a moment. Just need to check on the Special Agent. I know my way without going on the path."

Jenny looked at me with big eyes, "Ok but He did say to stay here and wait for him."

"I know but can't do it. He may be hurt out there and need help. Buddy is really good hunting dog so he will protect me." I was saying as I opened the back door. Buddy bounded out and pulled me down the steps and right into Special Agent Manchester. I tripped and he caught me. Our faces were inches apart. We stared into each other's eyes for a moment longer than we should, I thought he was going to kiss me, but instead he pushed me away, standing me up with his strong grip then backing up further he shouted, "What the hell, I told you to stay in the cabin!" Then seeming to gather himself he said much calmer, "Everything is under control. Please go back inside the cabin." He gestured to the back door and I pulled Buddy back into the cabin. I was starting to get mixed signals from this Special Agent and didn't like it. I am a straight forward person but have learned to wait for the right time to confront what needs to be confronted.

"So Special Agent Manchester I am glad you are alright. What were those gun shots we heard?" I said wanting answers. I will have to use self-control and boundaries with this guy.

"Thank you for your concern but I am a trained agent that can take care of myself and all of you. That is why I am here. I was close to the area you had seen something move Miss Marie and found foot prints. I scouted the area and finding nothing more, I let off a couple of shots to let whomever was out there know we are armed. I would like to get us all back to the town asap for better protection. It is only a short distance away to the town so let's get started. Buddy can lead with Miss Marie then Little Marie and then Jenny with me behind. If anything happens please do what I say. It will either be get down run and hide or just run. Do not worry about me I will take care of all of us." Special Agent Manchester was back to his controlled professional manner. He was very easy to trust when he was in that mode.

We walked the path back in the exact order Special Agent had demanded. Arriving at the Main street entrance to the town, with no problems. Waiting there was the deputy and his volunteers to escort all of us to the community center that was now set up for the FBI crew that was just now arriving.

Special Agent Manchester had a plan that he filled me in on once he had briefed the agents and had me wait for him at my small cottage down the street, on the corner of Main St. Ten minutes later I was being briefed in my living room.

"Miss. Marie, we have information that the "Boss man" knows you are here. We believe he has an informant that is here in your community. We want to take you back to Orcas island without anyone knowing you're going. We will have a decoy go by boat to Seattle with everyone thinking you are going to a safe house, but we will fly you in a helicopter to your Dad and Moms cabin. Call them while you pack, and I will back to take off in thirty minutes. I have a man right in front so no worries." He said with a wink then walked out the door closing it behind him.

"What was that? He is too good looking to be winking at anyone. It doesn't seem professional. I don't get him. Well I don't have to get him do I!" Saying this out loud to help my frustration. The problem was I was feeling something I have not felt in a long time and it was scary. Well going to see Mom and Dad was going to be great. Dialing Mom's cell phone, I walked to the closet to get my small bag I would need to pack. I have my own stocked cabin on the property now so no need to pack too much.

"Hello. Who's calling?" Mom answered.

"Hi Mom, it's me! How are you guys?" I said thinking that was weird she should know it was me with caller ID. "Can you talk?"

"Oh, hello dear. No this is not a good…" she paused a moment, I thought I heard someone in the back ground, then her somewhat more shaky voice came back on the phone, "Yes dear, now is fine. Thought something was burning on the stove. What do you need?"

"Well I am coming for a visit and wanted to make sure my cabin is ready. I have some important things to tell you and I need a break from Healing Wings." I replied a bit perplexed.

"Oh my, well let me see. OK, OK! Yes, that will be wonderful! But bring Buddy! I'm sorry dear but I do think something is burning on the stove. I've got to go now. We will all see you when you get here. Bye, Bye, dear!" she said and then the line went dead. Now that was weird. She doesn't cook but maybe the cook has a day off? Her voice was so strange, but she is getting up there in years maybe having an off day. And who it was, "the all" that I will see? Maybe some visitors but she would have told me?

I packed a few jeans and shirts. Then took a quick shower to be fresh for the trip. The doorbell rang exactly thirty minutes later. I think I surprised him being ready and having Buddy on his leash going also, because he looked me over then smiled saying "Nice to see you had enough time to freshen up." Then he seemed to catch himself and listen to his ear piece, "Ok, Miss Marie, we need to wait for the decoy so she can leave through the back door. She has been hiding somewhere. Ok she is here, "Where?" He asked while staring at me. "What in the bedroom. Why was that window not locked?" He barked.

Little Marie Grows Up

"Excuse me. I haven't had time to think about such things. Normally this community is safe! This has been a very long day I would appreciate it if you back down a little bit! And it would have been nice to let me know the decoy was going to hide in my house!" answering quite loudly. I had had it with his barking orders at me.

"I do apologize for that. I had no time to tell you the entire plan because it was still in the making. Also, I have to remember that this island is way out in the boonies with little crime. I am concerned for your safety." He smiled that smile again stepping closer. "Will you forgive me?" He reached out his hand and before I could shake it the decoy came into the room.

"Well James I see you have done it again. Hello Miss., I am Agent Stacey Gilroy. Sorry to have surprised you both!" The beautiful red head responded with a devilish grin on her face. Then she came over and got to business. "I borrowed one of your jackets and cap." Then she pulled a blond wig out of the small backpack she was carrying. Putting the wig on and then the cap you could not see her face to well.

I finally got my words back and replied, "Glad to meet you Agent Gilroy. There are no worries about any surprises, I'm starting to expect it around this guy! Help yourself to whatever you need and thank you for your help." Then to get a drink of water.

"Well James isn't she so sweet. I can see why you are so attracted to her, pretty lady." Agent Stacey said walking past him with a wink.

"Hey wait a minute Agent. First of all, you will address me as Special Agent Manchester, not James! Second, you have no idea about my attractions for anyone, which is none of your business. Third, you will be a professional and respectful FBI agent! Is that clear, Agent Gilroy." He said with complete self-control, I thought, smiling to myself, hearing everything. There must be something between those two, but none of my business.

"Yes Sir!" She saluted and added, "Ready when you are sir." Then she stood at attention.

"OK Gilroy, knock it off!" He ordered and then came into the kitchen. "Miss. Marie, I will be taking your decoy, Agent Gilroy to the boat to make it look like I am taking her/you to a safe house somewhere in Seattle. But I will not be going. I will be back in approximately 15 minutes. Here is an ear bud so I can talk to you and this pin is so you can talk to me. Put it in now, so we can test it." He handed me the two tiny pieces of spy ware. Now it was sinking in, this is really happening.

I started fumbling with the ear piece because my hands were shaking, I dropped it on the floor. I really had to face this danger and trust this man to protect me. At the same time, we both bent down to grab the ear piece and we grabbed it together, his hand over mine.

He spoke first, "You are shaking. It will be alright Miss. Marie, I am here. Let me help you with that." He helped me stand up, then gently brushed my hair back to be able to put the ear piece into my left ear. His touch ran shivers down my neck. I wanted to melt into his arms right then and there and let him protect me. Get over it Marie, get a grip.

I backed away from him to put the little pin on my shirt collar myself, replying "Why thank you but I can manage now. The reality just hit me of what is happening and the danger of it all. When you get back, I need to tell you about the weird conversation I had with my Mother." Remembering to think proactive and self-controlled in times like these.

"That sounds good. Can you hear this in your ear piece?" He was talking very softly.

"Yes. I can hear you. What about you, can you hear me?" I said just as soft.

"Yes. Ok we are leaving but I will still be able to hear you and the reverse is true." He said as he turned to the door and they left his arm holding Agent Gilroy's.

It was very comforting to know he could hear me, but very disconcerting. My feelings are all over the place. I felt jealous. What was happening with me? I know it's been a long time, but I was not even thinking of ever feeling for a man, this way again! I still can choose not to, right? Probably just a crush nothing more. Well that question had to wait. There are more important things to think about. My cell phone rang, and I picked it up to see Jenny was calling. "Hi Jenny, what's up?"

"Well we are having a problem with Beth. After she heard you were leaving to the safe house, she is refusing to eat or rest. She is sitting on the floor, in the corner, rocking back and forth, holding her little stuffed bunny calling out your name." Jenny finish with a gasp of air.

"Oh no, poor little thing. Can you with an agent walk her over to Charlotte's house next door, around back and then to my back door? Tell her you are bringing her here, but she needs to very quiet."

"Hello Miss. Marie, what are you doing? We do not have time for that. You hear me Miss. Marie?" Special Agent Manchester was repeating himself.

So, I acted like I could not hear him and told Jenny good bye. Then I said "Sorry, what was that? I could not hear you the ear piece thingy popped out of my ear when I was talking to Jenny. Poor little Beth is having a hard time without me, so I needed to talk to her before we leave. We will be done by time you get back. Don't worry." Telling a little fib and asking for grace for it.

"OK, OK but we will need to leave soon." He demanded.

"I hear ya. You will hear what we are saying anyways so no worries." That was something I had not thought about. Well it will be ok.

"Ok fine. See you soon." Was his reply.

I watched as Jenny and the agent with Beth went into Charlotte's house. Going to the back door to unlock it to let them in I remember to say a silent prayer. "Amen" I guess that was out loud because the special agent in my ear said, "Are you praying?"

"Now this is getting weird with you in my ear and listening to everything. I'm not sure I like it." I complained.

"Well you better get used to it because I am here until we catch the bastard!" he said very seriously. "It's my job and this is the way it's going to be. I will try to not be a pain." He chuckled then.

I chose to ignore him and opened the door to let Jenny and Beth inside. The Agent stayed in the back waiting to take them back. "Oh, sweetie so glad to see you." She ran to me almost knocking me over and clung to my waist.

"Please Miss. Marie don't leave me. I need to hear the rest of the story to know how to be brave and a hero like Little Marie. Please, please, don't go." She sobbed into my shirt.

"It's alright sweetie. I am here and will be back to finish the story, in a few days. We need to catch the bad man and then I will be back. Jenny will take good care of you." I tried to comfort her.

"NO, No I must hear the story before you leave. What if you never come back? Then who can tell me the ending? No! I want to come with you." She cried.

What was I supposed to do now? If I take her with us that could be putting her in danger but if I leave her now she may run away or worse hurt herself. She seemed so desperate. "Ok, sweetie we will think of something." I motioned for Jenny to leave Beth with me and she could leave. I just knew I had to bring her with us to the island. It was a very strong sense, so I made my mind up. The problem now was the Special Agent was now in my ear.

"Miss. Marie what are you planning?" Was ringing out loud and clear in my ear.

"Just get back here. I have a say in what I will and will not do. You have no idea what this little girl has been through and I am her only comfort right now. She is in a very vulnerable condition emotionally and my responsibility. You know how that feels. So, we will make this work, just hurry back, please!" I asked, then ask God to put it on Manchester's heart as well.

"I'm just around the corner. Be there in a sec." He came in the back door that Jenny just had left. "Ok what's the plan?"

"Well, we bring her with us. My mom will love to have her, and it will be a good place to finish the story I started for her." I was hoping he would not argue too much.

"What story is that? We have a lot of important things to do and it may be dangerous, but I think it will be alright with your family there, so ok. Let's get Buddy. Beth will have to behave to go. I have a back way planned to the hospital helipad. Hiking through the back yards of this town was easy because no fences higher than 3 feet or no fences at all, just beautiful landscaping connecting the yards. Little Beth was so happy she was coming with us. She held my hand and her bunny in the other hand, being as quiet as a church mouse, keeping up with us with no problems. She was a brave girl, she just did not know it yet!

"Ok, we are going to take the helicopter at the hospital. I will be back with an ambulance for you two to get in the back. We will make Beth the patient. Won't that be fun Beth?" Manchester asked.

"Oh yes I can pretend." She said shyly.

Little Marie Grows Up

"Ok I will be right back. Miss Marie can be the nurse." He said with a slight smile on his lips.

Waiting there I tried not to think of those lips and what kissing them may be like. Oh boy this was bad. I was going to have to keep guard of my mind. It would not be so hard to do if he wasn't so him! Ha, Ha, that's funny couldn't even say it was his looks anymore. There was something more and I was enjoying the long-forgotten feelings that attraction brings. But now, oh Lord help me!

He pulled up to the side of the road we were waiting on and jumped out to open the back doors. "We are in luck, there are some scrubs in the back. Put them on Nurse Marie. Beth here let me help you get up on the gurney. Please hold Buddy under the blanket. Ok one of the staff know what we are doing so they will help, and we will be in the air in no time. Sorry if this seems like a lot of trouble, but someone may be watching on the island or just off the island. We do know there is someone following the decoy but don't know if there are more out there." He said sincerely.

"I appreciate the reasoning, and this is somewhat fun in an odd way." I found myself saying.

He smiled and after putting on a white lab coat, he got in the front seat. He drove down the street then put the siren on and turned toward the hospital. I checked on Beth and she was laughing. She did like playing pretend. I did too at her age. I had to tell Buddy not to bay. Luckily, we were close by. We arrived and the doors flew open and two hospital staff rushed to help with the gurney. Boy it was like being in a movie. I tried to look the part. Special agent Manchester looked like a Doctor and we entered the hospital and up the elevator to the Helipad.

Within minutes we were up, up, and away. "This is my first time in a helicopter. So, you are a pilot as well as an FBI Special Agent? Jack of all trades." I said in my head set.

"Yes, I was a pilot before the FBI. And no not Jack, it's James of all trades." He laughed at that. "Ok we are on our way and should be there in 40 minutes. What was it you wanted to tell me about your mom?"

"Thank you for reminding me..." After explaining all the oddities of her part of the conversation ending with "and she said to bring Buddy? I always bring Buddy and she never has to tell me to. What do you think?"

"That is strange. I think we have to be on guard. Do you think someone was there with her? Maybe she was trying to tell you without them knowing?"

"Yes, that is what I am starting to think. Oh no, mom and dad could be in danger. What do we do now?" asking clearly shaken again. I needed to focus and pray. I know God is with me and them. He has given me this Special Agent and I need to trust you Lord. A little calmer I waited for his answer.

"I will have to think about that for a minute. I will call for back up but I think we need to still go but stay out of sight. First text your mom and tell her you are delayed and will be there tomorrow night. That should give us time to find out what is going on." His voice was calm and commanding which was very helpful at the moment. He radioed head-quarters while I sent the text to mom. "I hope she sees this text, she is not good about texting yet." I said to let him know I did what he requested.

"That is alright, she can call you when we don't show up tonight. I have back up coming in about an hour or two. We will be there first. Can we take a small boat to the end of the cove to get to your cabin?"

"Yes."

"Is there enough cover to be in your cabin without being seen from the main house?" was his next question.

"Yes and no. The back of my property can be seen from the side of the main house, but the front rooms face the end of the cove. We can keep it closed up looking for sure." I was happy to report.

"Good I will have a boat waiting close to the landing site. It will be there in ten minutes about 9:00 pm." He landed by a dock with a boat just pulling up for us. We all got on the boat and took off toward my cabin. Another five minutes later we were coasting up to the beginning of the cove, to beach the boat. It was dark now, but quarter moon gave enough light to see. My cabin was the last built here and I found a very nice location by the point. A short pathway through the trees lead to the front porch, I could just see enough to unlock the door and were all piled in Buddy first of course.

"I have some oil lamps we can use, and I will set up a bed for Beth. It is getting late."

"I am going to check things out. You three stay here no matter what you here. I will keep you update Miss. Marie." pointing to his ear piece, I nodded I understood.

"Oh, please tell me the story now Miss Marie?" little Beth begged.

"Well maybe just a little more, but then to sleep. Now let sit here on the couch. Where did I leave off?" I asked truly forgetting.

"Little Marie watched Fear scare the girls in the cave and heard Pride talking." Beth remembered.

"Oh yes." So, remembering Manchester could hear me, I started where Little Marie says....

Everyone Needs to be Rescued Sometime

"I guess that's what Pride does best. Looking like something he is not!" Little Marie thought as she watched him fly off with the group leaving Lies and Fear lurking down on the human group in the cave…

She is in her Fairy world.

But back in the real world in the real cave this was the scene that unfolded.

A worried Casper asked, "Captain Ray, you sure you want to wait the storm out in a cave? It might get flooded or something?" as they walked the precious live cargo into the cave and having them sit down on the damp sand along the back wall.

"This is a great place to hold up, so do what your told and without any more comments from you, Mr. Casper!" The Captain bellowed pulling out a bottle of rum, for himself. He walked over to the other side of the cave to take a swig of the golden liquid, calming his nerves a bit.

Burt already had a small fire going and the special bottle of water to give the girls to keep them calm. They would not be able to go without it in a few more days of drinking this stuff, without going through major withdrawals. He didn't want to be around when that happened, he thought then said, "Hey Casper get over hear and pour some water for the girls." Burt enjoyed bossing Casper around!

"Ok hold your horses!" Casper wanted to say a lot more but held his peace. As he bent over to give the first in the line a sip of "water" when the little one on the end stood up and scream then passed out and before he knew it there went another one and then another.

"What the hell!" Burt pushed past him making him spill some of the water. "What's going on here?" At his loud voice all the rest of the girls started to cry loudly. Without thinking Burt grabbed one of the girls and told her to shut up or he would make her shut up. "That goes for the rest of you, too!" He tossed her back to the floor and with a small whimper she sank back into line. "That's better. Casper get over here they need their water ration for the night." Burt went back to the front of the cave to cool off, he was a ticking time bomb and had to blow off some steam... "I'll be back... going to check on the storm." He almost ran out of the cave. Something about it made him uneasy.

Back in the fairy world Christina said, "Little Marie, I will be right back. You wait here, quietly." She then flew up and out a hole the lead to the base of the cross on Refuge Point. She flew as fast as she could to see where Brutal was going. She could see when he left it was because something was bothering him. Her love for him made her continue to try to show him the truth of love, mercy and grace. He still could choose the right path. Her hope drove her forward! Reaching the top edge of The Cliffs of Lies she called down, "Oh no don't go there Brutal!" Seeing him as he walked to the base of the cliffs. She was too high up. Too far for him to hear her. Her voice was not strong enough to be heard over the wind that blew along the cliff walls. She knew it had a way of twisting whatever was said in this place into lies, so it seemed hopeless calling down to him. With a wish and a prayer, she flew over the edge and down the side of the cliff straight toward her lost love. Only once the wind tried to deter her from getting to Brutal. "Whoo-shooo goesss thereee? Noooo One can make it passssssst here! I am powerful!!!!!" was what the gust of wind exclaimed, almost blowing her into the cliff side.

To the wind she shouted, "Only The I AM, The Creator God is more powerful! He is for me so who can be against me! Be Gone." At that she flew down to what felt like the last hope for her dear love. The wind went calm and at that moment Brutal could hear the truth, so Christina grabbed his paw like hand, to get his full attention. She spoke the truth of the forgiveness and love of the Creator Father. Through faith in the Son

Jesus Christ, The I AM gave us a way to be washed clean from all that separates us from, Them.

Brutal was so broken and ashamed of the terrible things he had done in the past that with no hope of ever being redeemed, he ran from the love of his life straight into darkness and pain of this twisted world he found himself in. Yet here she was telling him that he could be forgiven. Washed clean from all he had done or would do in the future. He paused, this gave him a hope that he had lost when he became this beast. Was this possible! Could he be healed? After all he had done to her and The Creator she was standing there forgiving him and loving him! This touched his broken heart and the horrid creature he had become. How does he receive this grace...? "What is the catch?" He heard himself saying.

"You must be willing to be changed to be like Them. Following the example of The Son with the help of the Holy Spirit you can become what you were lovingly created to be before you chose fear and lies. Causing you to do all kinds of foolish things. One of those things was leaving me! I love you and forgive you my love, Christopher...please come back to me." Christina kissed his hand and he fell to his knees.

"Oh, can this really be true. I can be truly forgiven... Oh let it be so! I do believe in The Son Jesus I was just so ashamed. I ran away from Him because of fear and shame, instead to Him. O please forgive me." Brutal cried out falling face down on the ground. When he stood up again it was not as Brutal but as the Count Christopher once again! Handsome and strong but for the one scar left across his right check reminding him of where he came from before he was saved. Christina held him to her and thanked God for the answer to her prayers.

Count Christopher looked around and realized they must leave before they were seen. "Go my love and we will meet at the gathering place. I have something to take care of before I can go with you. I will see your lovely face tomorrow at sunrise." He tipped her chin up to receive his kiss that sealed their hearts together forever.

"We have victory my love because of the Lord Jesus, always remember that!" Christina said while she flew up to the forest edge to go back to the spot, she left Little Marie.

Meanwhile Little Marie was almost ready to jump off the ledge she was hiding on, to attack Fear and Lies for all the tormenting they were doing to the girls and men in the cave. It was so obvious to her what they were doing but the poor girls could not see them. It seemed like they could hear them, though. Casper was ready to give another girl a drink when all of the sudden a big flash of lighting hit behind the cross on Refuge Point lighting up the cave through the hole Christina left through. Then thunder shook the cave and Fear and lies hid in the sides of the shadowy rock walls. The cross let up a shadowed outline separating the girls from the men. Again, another flash with thunder immediately following. Casper dropped the water and tripped over a rock in the sand trying to run from the fear that gripped him. While the Captain ran over and grabbed him up by the collar, "You fool how are we going to control these girls without that water!" yelling to be heard over the fierce storm that had suddenly hit. "Get some more from the boat and I'll watch them. And get that idiot Burt back in here, pronto!"

"Yes sir." Is all Casper replied, embarrassed, he didn't argue but once outside he thought better of this whole stinking deal! Maybe now is my chance to get away from this mess. But then remembering who he was running from because of the money he owed he thought again. So, looking down the beach toward the cliff at the middle of the cove he could see Burt come back fighting the driving rain and lighting that seemed to be hitting all around them. "What the hell are you doing out there, man! Are you crazy" Casper yelled through the sound of the storm, as Burt ran up to him.

"Never mind. We've got to go! Here let me help you with that." Burt took the bag of supplies Casper had gotten from the boat and they both ran for cover back in the cave.

※

Christy was starting to rock her sister so she would wake up. "Little Marie, wake up, wake up! We have to go!"

"Ok, OK…sorry good dream!" Little Marie replied with a yawn and stretch.

"Come on we need to hurry and go get Misty and Cindy. Mommy says there is a big storm coming and the FBI wants everyone to stay here while those guys are out there. We are going to go pick them up, so hurry up!" Christy called out while running out the bedroom door and down the stairs.

Oh no the storm! We need to hurry! Little Marie thought while jumping out of the bed and grabbing her necklace to put in her little backpack. "I have to tell them about the cove and the cave, but how? They will all think I'm crazy! Oh Lord help me to know what to say and do. Amen." Little Marie whispered and ran down the stairs with hope and excitement instead of Fear and Lies.

Mr. Paul, Mommy, and Christy were waiting in a SUV with a Lady driver that was introduced as Special agent Green with the FBI. Taking off toward Cindy's cottage, as soon as Little Marie buckled her seat belt, Special agent Green started to question her. "Hi there Little Marie, I was wondering if you could answer some questions to help us find those men who have those young girls?" She smiled looking in the rearview mirror. She could see the little girl sitting in the middle seat between the mother and sister. The Mr. sat in front.

"Yes, you may. I think I know where they are right now!" Little Marie announce with surprise to herself and everyone in the vehicle. "I mean ah I think they might be in a cave down in the cove with the cliffs all around it. I found it the other day. It looked like the spot they would take them ah maybe ah if there was a storm like this one coming here." She smiled back in the mirror at the agent.

"Well How in the world..." Mommy started then Paul interrupted "When did you..." Then Christy realizing her little sister needed help, spoke up and said, "We found it before they grabbed us, right Little Marie?" Christy bumped her sister's leg. Little Marie answered, "Why yes that was it. And I think I heard that big man tells the short man about the cave." The sisters held hands hoping the adults would believe them.

"Ok, girls I will let headquarters know to check it out, but it's more likely they are out to sea by now and if they get into international waters it will be difficult to stop them. Now where is this cove? Can you point it out on this map?" She handed the map to the back seat and almost immediately Little Marie pointed to the cove that looked like Refuge Cove. Then she said, "I know there is a secret way into the cave from the top just under a wooden cross."

Again, the car load of people was silent in surprise. "How do you know that?" *Mommy was the first to ask.*

Christy just sat there looking at Little Marie like now what are going to do? But with a smile Little Marie just said, "Jesus showed me in my dreams." *Well that did it. Everyone in the car smiled to themselves all thinking oh how sweet and innocent Little Marie was and now they would have to remember she was just a little girl.*

"Oh Ok" *they Agent Green said and then spoke into her walkie-talkie telling headquarters low priority but to send a couple of agents to check it out.* "I give you the details when we get to our destination, over and out." *Green continued on to the cut off Paul pointed too. Once they arrived at the cottage's long winding pathway leading to the two trees and flashes of lighting and ponding thunder hit the area. They had to hurry if they were to miss the pouring rain. They all jumped out of the SUV and followed the girls to the trees.*

"Where is the cottage, I can't see it. The path just goes past those huge trees growing at an angle into the old growth forest?" *Mommy stated what everyone else saw.*

The girls giggled and ran through the trees stopping at the ugly front porch. When the adults made it through the trees they were amazed and a little sadden by the dilapidated little house.

"I'm going to have to help fix this for Cindy." *Mr. Paul announced as the front door opened with Misty peeking out.*

"Oh, it just looks that way to keep people from bothering Cindy. Come in I was hoping you would get here soon. I don't like thunder and lightning." *Misty said just as a loud clap of thunder rumbled above the cottage. She jumped back and then laughed as they all piled into the quaint little room.*

"Where is Cindy my dear?" *Mommy asked.*

"Well, she left about an hour ago saying she had to check on someone at the cove and would be home in a bit. What is a bit? I thought it was shorter than an hour?" *Misty replied.*

With worried expressions the adults looked at each other, then Agent Green stated "I will look into this. You all stay here until I get back.

Special Agent Green ran back up to the SUV parked on the road and radioed in the new development of a blind lady named Cindy going to the cove. Maybe we should check that place out. I'm going to go up to the top of the point, send someone to meet me there and send a couple of agents down to the beach tell them to wait for further instructions."

"Got it. Hobbs and Jordan are going to be at the beach location. Paulson will meet you on the Point." Dispatcher Collins replied. "Also, the coast guard has found a ship headed for international waters from Orcas and they have just boarded. Checking the cargo and paperwork. Will keep you updated, Sir."

"OK, I'll let you know if we need back up at the cove or if this is a dead end! Over n out." Green drove off in four-wheel drive knowing the road was going to be rough the next mile or so. She had been to the place Little Marie had spoken of and did notice a rocky area that she now wanted to investigate. It was strange when the little girl mentioned the cross she knew exactly where it was which made her feel something in her gut that something just might be going on in that cave. After following that character Casper to Orcas Island a few months ago she had had enough time to explore most of the island. It was her way at staying in touch with her surroundings to be in control when all hell broke loose, which always did in her line of work. She knew from very young she would have a life full of conflict and pain. She had chosen to be strong and smart and never the victim again. Working hard to be top of her class and getting away as fast as she could from home when she was 18. Becoming a Special Agent in the FBI was her way of proving she could do something to make all the men out there, the creeps and abusive ones, pay for their crimes! When this assignment came up she jumped at the chance to bring down a known sex trafficking ring in Portland Oregon. These were the worst of the scum out there she thought. Praying on girls that were weak and vulnerable because men couldn't control themselves. Well it has to stop and she was the one going to help bring these criminals to justice. She pushed the gas pedal down to get the SUV up and over a steep area before climbing up over the top of the ridge, stopping at the end of the dirt road next to the river where the vehicle Paulson already had parked there. At this point she would have to hike in.

Little Marie Grows Up

"Paulson come in! Paulson are you there?" Green called in her radio while hiking to the cross.

"I'm here Agent Green. I just found what looks like an entrance to a cave up here by a wooden cross.

I'm going in to check it." Paulson replied.

"That's a negative Paulson. I'll be right there, wait for me." Special Agent Green didn't like this new guy. He didn't respect her being in charge and she had to get him to understand who he was dealing with. "You hear me Paulson." The wind and thunder were getting worse as she rounded the edge of the tree line to see Paulson looking down the rocky hole with the lighting lashing just behind the cross that was placed there years ago. He jumped almost falling down the path that seemed to appear in the flash of the lightning. Getting up off the ground when Special Agent Green approached made her smile and he didn't like that but what could he do but shake it off. He would show her up soon enough.

"Hey there Paulson, you need help?" She came up behind him and past him to look down the path. "This could be pretty dangerous when it starts raining. Have you heard from Hobbs or Jordan?"

"Yes and no." He murmured. "They called in and reported seeing activity at an opening to a cave and went to investigate at a distance since we were all waiting for you." He smiled when she glared back at him. "But then a big flash and boom, the radios went silent. I've tried for about a minute now."

"Ok then we need to check this out. Stay close behind me and watch your step. Stealth mode now!" She started down the rocky path that had perfect steps carved into the rock giving them an easier time then she thought. As they came around a left corner it opened up unto a ledge overlooking a large cave about twenty feet down to the bottom. They both fell silently to the ground when they heard voices then a scream and then another scream. They bellied over to the edge to peer down to see 18 girls from the age of 5 to 15 chained up together. They were crying and a few looked like they had passed out along the left side of the cave. Two men, one looked like that goofy Casper she had thought might be part of this, were arguing and then Casper ran out of the cave.

"What do you want to do Green?" Paulson asked ever so quietly.

"You wait here, and I'll try Hobbs one more time and then radio for back up. Record this if you can, I'll be right back." She was gone before he could say a thing. He pulled out his camcorder and fixed to night mode he could zoom in on the Captain below to watch and wait for orders.

Green raced back up the steps to be right at the opening of the secret entrance. "Hobbs Come in Hobbs you there?"

"Yes here! Two men going back in … cave….. what……ders…… storm…..every….." Hobbs came in and out on the radio.

"Calling for back up now. Hold Position…Hostages… wait….!" Crackling and thunder roared. Special Agent Green then turned her attention on getting back up there and back down to the cave to save those girls.

"Collins come in. we need back up 18 young girl hostages in the cave. Did you get that! Collins…." Green was realizing with the storm she wasn't going to get through so not wasting any more time she went into get er done mode. She swiftly ran back to where Paulson was recording and told him her plan but before she could put it into action things began to change drastically.

"What the hell are you two doing out there! Get in here now and help me with the girls!" Captain Raymond bellowed a little unsteady on his feet.

"We are coming Cap'n Sir!" Casper yelled into the cave, "Burt will be right behind me." Casper came up to the fire light trying to distract the old man from noticing Burt coming up around to get behind him with a club.

"Hey there Big fellow what you up too coming up behind me like that!" Raymond slurred out. The Captain was a crafty old man, even when drinking. He saw the shadows on to his right. Stumbling to his left, he turned and pulled out his revolver. "Just hold it right there Bertie boy! Ha, didn't see that coming did you. Now get over there with Casper and give those brats some of that their water!" Pointing his gun at Burt then Casper.

"Now wait a minute Captain Ray, we are on your side and I was just bringing you some more of your favorite drink." Burt back up dropping the still hidden club in the sand and holding up a bottle in his other hand. The perfect lie at that moment he concluded as he watches the Captain stumble toward him trying to put the gun back in its place but missing

Little Marie Grows Up

the holster. "Ah sorry my boy I should know I can count on you, especially with what I have on you." He chuckled while reaching for the bottle with his free hand.

Burt took advantage of the Captain's miss guided stammering and went into action grabbing the gun first, then hitting the bottle on the top of the old man's head. At that moment the gun went off, Burt and the Captain fell to the ground with Burt on top. Neither one moved.

Then crying and screaming burst out from the girls watching in terror the seen unfolding before their Casper dropped the water, spilling it everywhere, and ran to see who had been shoot. Burt rolled over onto his back and then sat up winching. Captain Ray just laid there with blood pouring from his head and hip. Burt tried to stand but there was a burning pain in his leg and realized he had been shot, so he stayed down. Casper ran over to help but he pushed him away, "No, No! Go help the girls. We need to let them go. After the storm calms down, we can take them to Paul's place, drop them off and get lost!" Burt checked his leg out, it wasn't too bad, looked like the bullet just grazed it. He tied his sweatshirt around it and got up.

Casper was unlocking the girls and telling them he was letting them free, when Agents Hobbs and Jordan ran in the cave guns drawn and demanding everyone to freeze "FBI"!

Everyone froze and in minutes the cave was filled with agents taking them into custody and helping the girls to safety!

Special Agent Green handled coordinating all the details, first getting the girls to the local hospital to be checked out. "Now that the wind has calmed a little, we can get these girls to Island Hospital. Agents Kline and Treck, you are in charge of the girls. Jordan and Hobbs, we are taking these guys to interrogation!"

"Yes, Sir... ah Mam?" Agent James was new to the detail.

"It's Sir." Special Agent Green was used to that kind of confusion. Now that women where in jobs only men once had it had been difficult for them to know how to address the women. Sir is her choice because it is the authority, she earned becoming a special agent and head of this investigation. She walked over to the two live kidnappers, "Looks like you have a wound? Well doesn't look to bad so I think we can patch you up long enough to have a little chat." Before Burt could answer she walked

away to make sure everything was being handle by procedure, seeing that it was, she left Agent Jenkins in charge of the crime scene and body. She then walked out of the cave to get to the temporary set up of headquarters at Paul's house, thankful to Little Marie for helping her find the girls. The storm was starting to calm down to just a breezy, rain, at the moment so the trip back was easier...

"Well Beth it is late and there is a little more to the story, but it can wait. This is a good place to stop. The girls are rescued." I said while I carried her to the little bed I made in the corner of the room.

"OK, Miss Marie. I am so glad they believed Little Marie and saved the girls. Uhm I was wondering if you are Little Marie all grown up?" Beth asked with a yawn.

"Well yes I am, and I needed to remember some of the things that I had forgotten." I was happy she was able to be comfortable with me. "You are an answer to a prayer my dear and I thank the I Am for you! Now get some sleep. See you in the morning." I pulled the blanket up on her and she smiled while she snuggled her little bunny that seemed to be always by her side. Then closed her eyes, falling fast to sleep.

"Now that was very interesting." Manchester was in my ear again. Now what's he going to say about the story. "I did hear something about Little Marie helping Special Agent Green. Your going to have to tell me more. I am on my way back." He said with a bit of sarcasm.

"Well if you can hear me why wait?" I snapped back. I was a bit annoyed that I forgot he could her me.

"No problem. We needed to talk about that time anyway. It was sweet how you are telling Beth. It is good for her to know brave Little Marie." He answered much more serious.

"It's funny but I really have not thought of it for a very long time and I have never told the story quiet in this detail before. It is hard for most people to believe so I just never told it all before." I said as he quietly knocked on the door.

"It's me. Please unlock the door." Is all he said.

I opened the door as well as unlocking it, then walked back to the couch I was sitting on. This would be interesting. How he will react, to my Fairy world dreams and my experience's, that I know are real. I was not expecting to get into all this with him. I was going to stick to the basics and leave out those details. But now he heard me telling about the cave seen with Lies and Fear and Pride. What must he think? Why do I care? Stop it Marie you need to be true to yourself so don't worry about him. My thoughts were racing.

He walked over and sat across from me, asking "Ok so Special Agent Green said she wants to be called Sir, Burt is superficially wounded, and the girls were rescued. Can you tell me about what happened after that?" He recounted with a smile that turned serious with the question he asked.

A tiny bit relieved he didn't ask about her dreams, "Well, ok. This is what I remember from talking to Agent Green years later." I decided to start where I left off with Beth.

Special Agent Green was so invigorated now that the girls were found. She couldn't wait to get these bad guys into the interrogation room they had set up back at Paul's cabins. Well this was going to be the break she needed to get to the head man of this bunch of hoodlums. She had no doubt these two and the dead captain where not the leader of this Sex trafficking ring. "Well this has been a great day! I've got to get to the bottom of this. And these two are going to help!" She thought driving back to the cabin with a serious, determined smile on her face.

─────※─────

She briefed us back at the cottage "We found the girls! They are being taken to the Island Hospital, and we are dealing with the two we have in custody. Unfortunately, one man was dead before we got there. Let's all go back to the Paul's cabin I will fill you in. The storm has settled down and we should get back." Sp. Agt. Green noticed the panicked look Cindy had on her face so decided she wanted everyone back at the cabin so she could question her as to what she was doing out in the storm and what she meant by NOW everything will be ok! "Yes, I mean everyone. We don't know the whole story, we don't know if there are any more suspects on the loose, so we want everyone under one roof. Thanks! Now let's go people."

She spoke with the command she had learned to use to get her job done. Everyone hopped to it and helped Cindy close up the cabin safely.

Everyone was thoughtful on the way home but no one talked. It seemed like Agent Green wanted it that way. It wasn't hard even for Little Marie, who seemed to be dozing off in the middle seat, but everyone was relived and tired with shock lingering the air!

Little Marie was thanking Jesus as she rested next to her mommy. Saying a prayer for the girls and looking forward to getting back to the cabin, her necklace and bed...

Back at one of the small cabins Jordon and Hobbs separated the suspects for interrogation. Burt was right. It was only a superficial graze wound that one of the agents had a medic bandage up. "Don't want our prize to end up with an infection, do we!" Hobbs said laughing as Burt winched when the medic cleaned the wound.

After Special Agent Green debriefed the family in the main cabin, she joined Hobbs and Jordon in the smaller guest cabin to make a plan for the interrogation. But found that was not going to be needed because Burt had already asked to write his confession and Casper is cooperating. So, he was the first one she wanted to talk to anyway!

"So, Mr. Casper Cousins, no pardon me isn't it Mr. C. Gordon? No, no, what's wrong with me it is Mr. Casper Stevens." She walked around him looking him in the eye as she did and back behind and back in front again while she revealed his known alias's. He couldn't look into those beautiful blue green eyes, so he looked down at the table. She finally sat down in front of him after putting the jacket, she just took off, on the back of the chair. She leaned forward and asked, "So what is it, Casper?"

He looked up and kept silent for a minute. She was sure pretty he thought but she doesn't know it. She is so tough but once you looked deep enough you see the guarded softness. Oh no Casper stay focused here this is serious, and she is FBI! Wait come to think of it she looks kind of familiar. "Have we met?" He spoke up for the first time.

"Not that I know of Mr. Casper. Now do you want to tell me what you were doing in that cave with 18 tied up kidnapped girls, a dead Captains

Little Marie Grows Up

body and Mr. Burt C. Chasen?" She back away from his gaze that seemed to cut through her.

"That my dear is a long story! I guess now is as good as any time would be at this point." He Smiled showing a rugged handsomeness that gets lost in his usual somber expression.

She sat back in her chair and corrected him. "I am not your Dear! I am Special Agent Green and I am here to get the scum that kidnap girls and sells them in sex trafficking business! So, you are correct in one thing it is a very good time to tell Your story. My recorder is charged and ready.

"Well that sounds fine to me. I'm sick of that son of a bitch and what he has been holding over my head these past few years! May I have some water please? Also, I may need some protection after we are done talking." He smiled again and winked.

What the hell she thought, as she got up to get Hobbs to bring in some water. I don't like how he looks at me. "Get this guy some water I'm getting the story! So, your water is on its way. What's your story?" She pulled the chair out and turned it around to straddle it and listen to this perp's story. What she didn't realize sitting that way didn't help him any seeing her as a Special Agent. More like …. Snap out of it man, Casper had to bite his lip.

Hobbs came in with the water and sensed the awkward energy in the room and decided to stay if Green allowed it. What do you know, she motioned him to sit down. "Score, this will be interesting." He thought. Most the time they have a way to watch the interrogation but out here in the field it doesn't always happen even though they are video recording it.

"Ok you got your water and recording is going, now is the time to talk." She motioned to the recorder on the table.

"Ok Mam. Here you go. A few years ago, I got into some loan shark problems. I moved in with my widowed sister and her daughter to try to get ahead and pay it back. I got a good job and started saving but the thugs I owed were getting pretty restless. One night they found me at the local pub and threaten to hurt my sister and her kid if I didn't pay them by the end of the month. I told them take it out on me not my family, but they said that was stupid then I wouldn't be able to pay up. So, I was desperate to get the money. I had save $2000,00 but had $3000.00 more to go. As I was sitting there contemplating all the stupid things I had done, when Mr.

Burt C. Chasen, the name he gave me, sat down beside me at the bar. He started to tell me how I could make some extra cash in the next few days just talking to pretty girls. He didn't tell me anything about why. Well, I was getting drunk and was desperate, so I didn't ask. At first, anyway." He stopped to take a sip of water.

"So good old Burt was waiting right there for an opportune time for a down on his luck half way decent looking young man to be at that pub. Very interesting" Hobbs threw in his thoughts.

"Let the man tell his story Hobbs!" Green gave the look to be quite and motioned for Casper to continue.

"Now that you say that, it was kind of weird how he was there at the right time. I had never seen him hang out there before. Yes, I was becoming a regular. It was a place to chill after work. Anyways I went home with the instructions to meet up with Burt the next day. I didn't make it because my sister and niece were in a terrible car accident. I was a wreck. Was I the cause? My little niece died, and my sister lost her eyesight. Cindy was my top concern now, so after a few days I went back to the pub to look for Burt. I found him there, just like he was waiting for me, no one else. He told me, he heard from the bartender about the accident and understood why I stood him up, so he wanted to give me another chance because he felt sorry for me. I was thankful because with the medical bills for my sister and those goons still wanting their money, I was needing cash fast. I went to work for Burt and someone he called the Boss man. I never really met him, but I do think I saw him once. And yes, I will give you a description, but I don't know his name! As the months went by Burt introduced me to his friend Paul, who had a place on Orcas Island that my sister could stay and rebuild her life. I jumped at the chance trying to keep her away from any harm ever again!" At that he stopped and put his hand up to his forehead while slowly shaking his head, "I'm so sorry, sis. It's all my fault!" he whispered very softy only Agent Green heard him.

"That is a very sad story, if true, but please go on. You can rest when you are done." Green managed a small smile.

"Ok, well you can check it out so why would I lie? Cindy my sister..." Ah now I am seeing how Cindy fits into this picture, Green smiled to herself. "...lives here but I had no idea that this was the Island where the Boss Man, has his hide out. Burt's friend Paul has been very nice to us but

Little Marie Grows Up

maybe there is a reason? I don't know if he knows about any of this, but he sure has been helpful to us. I found out after being in to deep what they were planning for these girls and I've been wanting out ever since. I'm not a bad man just lost and confused after making a few bad choices. I am ready to face the consequences of my actions, but Burt and I planned to let the girls free and this is what happen in the cave. I went in to distract the drunk Captain and Burt was going to grab and tie the Captain up." He sighed and stopped for a moment.

"So, what was the change of heart for Burt?" Green asked.

"I don't quite know, but he was out in the storm walking back to the cave from the cliffs at the base of the cove. Thunder and lightning were all around and he was struggling to get back because of the driving wind and rain. He had to yell over the storm telling me his plan to let the girls go and I agreed. I was so done with this mess I had gotten myself into. I was so glad to have help finally, but it was strange that it would be the same guy who got me into this fix. He seemed so different, but we didn't have time to chit chat with the storm ragging and the girls still in danger inside the cave. When we went in, as I said, I was supposed to distract the captain and Burt was going to grab him to tie him up, but the Captain saw Burt coming up behind him and pulled his gun pointing it back and forth, at both of us. Burt quickly calmed the captain down and showed him a bottle of whiskey. The Captain went to grab it while Burt grab for the gun and raised the bottle hitting the Captain on the head. The gun went off and they both fell. I didn't know who had been shot until Burt rolled over and the Captain didn't move. Burt yelled at me to unchain the girls but then you guys came in and the rest is history!" Casper swallowed the last of his water with relief he had finished his confession, put the glass down and waited for a response from the beautiful FBI agent, now standing across the table from him.

"Well Mr. Casper that is a very interesting story and yes we will check it out. Right now, your buddy Burt is writing his confession. Here is some paper and a pen for you. Also, I will send in the sketch artist we have here and see if we can find the Boss man!" Special Agent Green put her Paul back on and added, "Thank you, for your honesty." She walked past Hobbs and gave him some instructions, then walked out of the door to get some *more answers to some new questions, Cindy would be a good start, before having a talk with the owner of this property Mr. Paul!*

I then stopped, realizing I had been telling the Special Agent Manchester this as a story like I had been doing with Little Beth. "Oh my. I apologize I was still in story telling mode. You probably just want the facts. I mean the facts are in there!"

"I think I can find the facts in there somewhere and I do enjoy how you tell a story." He said with a wink. There it was again his very disarming look, then it was gone. "Ok Miss. Marie from my investigation so far I have enough "facts" for now. I need to tell you what I found, or should I say not find when I went to the main house." He waited for a moment then went on. It seemed he expected me to react, so I just sat and listened. I knew I needed to use what I remembered today, that God is always with me to protect, guide and comfort me. He is my strength. "The house was empty, with only one light turned on inside. Finding no sign of anyone I found my way inside and to the room with the light, finding a note left on the desk addressed to Little Marie. Of course I opened it carefully, not to smudge any finger prints, it said "Little girls that don't do what they are told get hurt! Come to the cave in the cove! Alone." I almost did not tell you the Alone part because that will not be happening." He finished as he looked into my eyes.

Just sitting there absorbing the information, I wonder what he saw. I was hoping self-control because Fear was trying to break me with Lies right behind, but this time I used the truth that God Almighty was for me and with me, so I could trust the uncertainties with His truth not the worlds worries! That thought gave me courage again like all those years ago when I was Little Marie and first met Jesus the Son and the I Am. He has told me the power is in His word and the authority that I have to use it in His name. The Holly Spirit is whom He gave me, and I must rely and focus on Him. My mind still spinning I had not responded to Manchester yet. Then before I knew it, I was saying, "Oh yes, I need to find my necklace!" which was a very odd thing to say after being told about the note and my parents are missing.

Manchester said "Ok, we can try to do that, but I think we need to have a plan of action before the back-up agents gets here making it harder to be "alone" as the note suggests. We have about forty minutes.

They are coming in quiet and will meet us here." He then reached out and touched my arm, "Are you alright, Marie." Leaving off the Miss for the first time.

"I am alright, only because I know, they are with me." Was my answered.

He started looking around and then said "Who are you referring too? We are the only ones here."

"Them- The I Am- God the father, Jesus the Son and The Holy Spirit. They are with me and for me. Don't you know them Special Agent Manchester? They love you too. You are their creation also." I found myself saying the truth and did not care if he thought I was a religious freak. "Well when I was Little Marie, I experience Them and I needed reminding so I could face this trial with strength and peace." I finished my reply, hoping he would understand.

"Oh yes, I do know what you mean. I do not usually talk about my spiritual beliefs on the case, but yes, I am glad we have, Them, to lean on. Now about the plan. I am guessing the cave in the cove, is the one the 18 girls were rescued from? You know about a secret entrance from the report I read. That is to our advantage." He then did something special! He prayed with Me before we came up with a plan.

"I do really think my necklace is important. I think it is somewhere here in a box my mom brought over from the main house. I think I stacked them in the closet. Look there they are!" I was hoping to find my little back pack and the box I kept all my treasures in. This first box had some my baby and toddler clothes and shoes. But the second box we found both the backpack and treasure box. Nothing was in the backpack, so I looked in the box. It was stuffed full of birthday cards and little treasures, but the necklace was not there. "I do know where else I would have left it? I was a teenager when I last saw it in this box. Well, I guess I will find it if I am supposed to." I helped pack everything back and put the boxes in the closet again.

When the Agents arrived, we meet them at the porch to brief them on the plan. One agent was left to protect Beth and be home base for the team of four that included Manchester and myself. They geared me up with a bullet proof vest and flash light. I kept the ear piece in also.

"Ok everyone any questions? We only have one chance to get this done with no casualties." Special Agent Manchester asked looking at each one of us. We all did a thumbs up. Then with a wave and a nod we all took off to the cove. I went with Manchester in the Jeep and the other two took the boat and some diving gear.

I directed the Special Agent to the top of Refuge Cove past the Cliff of Lies I thought remembering very clearly now my Fairy world and even the feeling of being a little fairy myself. Very strange but never the less real. "Turn right, up ahead and go to the very end of the road, at the top of the cliffs. I hope it is still there. It's been a long time since I have been up here. Ok, park here. We will have to walk in from here." My heart was beating fast now with anticipation of the path and cross still being there. He stopped me at the edge of the tree line, making sure we were not being watched. Seeing it was all clear we quietly walked toward the point and the clouds parted with the moon revealing the wooden cross just were it was back when we rescued the girls but without a terrible storm. The clouds hid the moon again as we approached the rocks that created the secret entrance. "It's still here praise God!" I whispered. Smiling up at Manchester. He smiled back and gestured no talking as we went down into the caves back entrance. I nodded and he followed close behind me. I held my flash light down to see the rocky cave path. It was the same as I remembered. We came to the fork in the cave, for a split second, I wanted to go right, to investigate the path that led to the cliff face with the invisible opening, I now remember flying through. But Mom and Dad are the focus tonight, so I veered left to go to the ledge so we could spy on what was happening down in the heart of the cave. We crouched down crawling to the edge. There was a lantern placed on a flat rock near where Mom and Dad were sitting on the sandy floor tied together back to back. Way above them was a very large log hanging by a rope that looped though a ring that was attached to the ceiling of the cave, then it came over to another ring close to the wall and looped twice through, then down the cave wall to disappear under the sandy floor towards the cove entrance of the cave. "Looks to me like a trap and something to be very careful of when down there." I whispered ever so slightly.

All of a sudden, we heard voices coming into the cave, "Hey you know the Boss man has lost it. This is proving it with his revenge against these people. I am not liking this right now!" The skinny tall man said to the short balding man.

"I know, I know. He has not been sleeping and the doctor has him on all kinds of stuff. Just one more night. We will be rich and free of him. Just don't let him hear about it. He may be a has been, but he still has connections that are in the Family if you know what I mean. He will be crazy so let's get to it." The bald man replied. They went to separate corners of the cave and hid themselves behind camouflage blankets.

Thinking to myself. Well that's not going to help them I thought. Oh Lord thank you. I know we have Your help.

Then another loud raspy voice erupted through the silence toward the entrance, "You boys here hiding? Oh yes, I sees ya both, but had to be looking for ya. That Little Marie bitch is not gonna notice you at all! When she sees her poor Mommy and Papa tired up here unconscious, with this here log, just waiting to fall down and crush them before her very eyes!" He coughed out, trying to laugh. Clearing his throat, he continued, "She will be wishing she never messed with me!" He walked over and kicked my Dad, who didn't move, but I heard Mom groan, as she felt the blow to her husband's body. He finally turned around so we could see his face. It was the first time seeing this so called "Boss man". He was average height and build. The shadows in the cave gave him an angular look to his long face and nose to match. He wore a baseball cap over his somewhat long white wavy hair. His white beard and mustache were trimmed short, surrounding his narrow lips. His eyes were the scary part of his face, set a little too far apart with an empty darkness in them, that could be seen even at this distance.

Then in a quieter voice he said, "We are waiting Little Marie it is time for you to pay. Boys she will be here soon, and we are gonna have some fun." He laughed at that, then another cough. "I will be waiting at the entrance."

Thanking God, the mad man did not get the text I sent Mom, thinking this was it! Time to face the enemy! But not alone! We crawled back to the path and to a safe place not to be heard.

Special Agent Manchester then started excitedly explaining a new plan. "We now have a better option. I will go down to the hiding boys and take care of the big one closest and if I can get to the other one I will but if not, we can handle the Boss man and him, with the agents posted outside the cave. I will be hiding in one of the blankets. So, when you come in, I will be there to cover you. You got it?" He stopped seeing my face, "Are you alright?" He must have seen the anger there because I was fuming. That man down there was who had caused all the pain in my life. He was the reason my life has been haunted. He took my love away and now I'm having to recue my parents from him! It has been so many years fighting fear, due to him. I knew I was looking at pure evil, standing there in the flesh. I wanted to kill him at that moment and that scared me most of all.

Facing the Boss Man

With a shaky voice I announce, "I don't know if I can do this? He is the one who has brought so much misery into so many lives, and to see him there using my parents to hurt me, I just want to kill him! What if my dad is already dead! He didn't move or anything when that terrible man kicked him?" I couldn't say anymore because that was the question that was the most terrifying to me. No way could I live with myself if this monster kills them. With that I started to burst into tears. All the reality of it all, that has caused my pain, was from one evil man and he was down there, right now waiting to cause more pain was a bit overwhelming to say the least.

With ease, Special Agent Manchester pulled me into his arms and held me for a moment giving me time to process what was needed to be processed but only for a moment. He softly said as he let me go to wipe my tears. "Miss. Marie, I do really understand this is a very stressful time but just knowing you for 24 hours, I know you can do this. I would not ask you if you could not. We would be doing this a completely different way, if I didn't believe in you." He stepped back a bit father as if he needed to compose himself also. That made me smile. "Good I knew you had it in you! Now let's get this done. Remember all the things we talked about when dealing with this guy." He waited for my reply.

"Thank you, Special Agent, I appreciate the confidence and you are right I can do this. This battle needs to fight, but I know I am not alone! I am ready. The side path to get down to the cove and then to the entrance will take about eight minutes. See you in eight to ten minutes, praying for you taking care of those two hiding." I replied getting ready to walk up and out to the cross entrance. He followed until he saw me get to the top. The clouds moved shinning moonlight to be able to see him hold up his hands in a prayer motion changing to a thumbs up, then he disappeared back into the cave.

I walked to the path with the moon light still guiding me. The pathway was along the tree line and the cliffs. Memories flooded my mind as I walked down to the cove. As if on que the clouds covered the light of the moon as I stepped onto the beach. I still did not need my flash light and decided not to use it. Maybe the Boss Man would not see me coming. Keeping myself focused on the plan and the truth I was not alone, I walked up slowly keeping in the shadows as best I could. Then there he was standing there waiting to finish his evil plan, well I knew what was meant for evil against me, God will turn into good. With that as my strength, I popped out from the shadows and relished in the fact I almost gave him a heart attack right there and then. "Hope I scared you, you old coot!" I yelled out so Manchester could hear me.

"What the Hell! You bitch!" He bellowed, then coughed. "You won't be doing that again. Now you will get in here, if you know what's good for you! Or should I say your Mommy and Daddy. Little Marie!" He demanded.

"First off, I will tell you something, you bastard! I am Marie and it only looks bad for you that a little girl was your downfall! So just keep using the Little for my name, it keeps showing how foolish you are. The power doesn't come from me anyway. It comes from the I Am. The Creator Father God, The Son Jesus the Christ and the Holy Spirit. Against Them you are fighting." I was surprised at what I was saying and even more so that it had made him back up a step, shaking.

"You don't come here spouting your religion. There is no one to help you here. I made sure of that. Your two FBI agents are all tied up over there. No one left but us. Waste time if you want. Your parents are in there dying or dead for all you know, and you are sitting here preaching at me. Suit yourself. I have time they don't!" He spat back at me.

"Why don't you lead the way, Boss man?" I asked.

"No, no! I insist you first, Marie." He replied.

"Ok if you insist." I walked into the entrance. Looking for any sign of where the rope for the booby trap was lying.

"Why are you walking so slow? Move it." He then pushed me forward. I saw a small lump of sand covering something just in time to jump and then tripping falling to the cave floor. "What are you doing, get up and look over there." He said pointing to were both my parents were laying. I acted surprised and notice only one camo blanket being used. Oh, Praise Jesus!

"Mom! Dad are you OK?" I cried out to them. They did not move. I started to walk closer and his raspy voice stopped me in my tracks.

"Lookie, there? What is up there. I wonder what will bring it down?" He said while hanging on to the rope. "Since you didn't trip on it, I can just let er go and splat. That would be that. Now who has the upper hand missy. You have been so confident, but you didn't know who you were up against. Little Marie did take something from me, and I will get my revenge. But by no means did that ruin my life like I have yours!" He was relishing in his final plan coming to an end. "I have waited a long time for this and now before I go, I am given a chance to finish it!" He coughed out.

"You have wasted your time. Yes, you have hurt me, but I am overcoming that with love and forgiveness. I realize now that is what you need. Forgiveness. You don't know it yet that does not matter to me, I need to do it so I will be free of you! Only then will I heal and become stronger! So, I forgive you, Boss man. I forgive you." I truly was relieved saying that, but it only seemed to torment him.

"What! You can't do that! I don't need anything from you or your religious ways!" He fell to his knees still holding the rope.

"Everyone needs forgiveness. It's grace not religion!" I said, again surprised at what I was saying.

There was power in those words. While I was talking, Special Agent Manchester was pulling my parents from under the log. I continued to distract the Boss man so he would not let go of the rope. But just then the Boss man starting yelling for his men to shut me up. When the men did not respond, he realized what was happening.

"What the hell." He said as he let go of the rope.

I screamed out, "NOOOOOOO!", while Jumping for the rope, but missing it, the log came crashing down. The sound of the rope ripping through the rings and then the bang as the log hit the cave floor, made me scream again. I ran over to see the damage, holding my breath waiting as the sandy dust cleared and was so relieved to see Mom and Dad resting against the wall with Manchester lying flat out, right next to the log. He was on his feet in no time and on the Boss man before the guy could escaped, while he was tying him up, as I was untying my parents and trying to revive them. Oh, praise God they are alive.

"Marie I will be alright, but I think Paul needs help. They roughed him up and may need to go to the hospital." Mom was saying when Dad winched and said, "No I'll be alright just get me back to the house."

"We will decide what both of you need. Now rest and we will have help here soon." I said then pulled Manchester outside to show where the other agents were tied up.

"Well, what happened here? You guys ok?" The special agent said after cutting off their ties.

"It will be in our report, Sir." Is all that was said.

"Ok. I will look forward to reading it. Now if you can manage it please call for the coast guard, we have injured people in there. Also get the prisoner in the boat and back to base camp ASAP. We got some interrogating to do." He said sarcastically.

"I'm going to wait here with Mom and Dad. Then I will be back at my cabin when they are settled and ok. Well you let Little Beth know I will be back later." I said with a shaky voice.

Reaching out to me he said, "Sure thing, Marie. It's all over. Everyone is ok. You did so good back there. I'm, proud of you." He said standing just a few inches from my face with his hand on my shoulder. I almost leaned in to kiss that wonderful mouth saying such kind things as he looked at me like that! What was he waiting for? Confused, I turned away and ran into the cave finding it hard to let my heart go again. Fear of pain that comes from loving a man and hoping for a future. Yet we just caught the man responsible for that pain and I was not given a spirit of fear but of power, love and a sound mind. I will have to learn to trust anew.

Well after a few hours Dad and Mom went in the hospital recovering from scrapes and bruises. Dad had a concussion, so they were going to keep him over night. Before I left Mom had me sit close and whispered, "I found this the other day in Christy and your old room. It was under your bed, hidden in the crack of the floor board. I thought you would want something so beautiful. Thank you for being there always. Love you my, Little Marie." She kissed my hand and handed me a small box.

"Thank you, Mother dear. I will let you sleep, now." She had already closed her eyes while I opened the box. Could it be. I hope it is... Yes! It's the necklace and was more beautiful then I remembered.

I wonder? No, I can't do that here because I will be sleeping and need to lay down. Plus, someone will have to wake me up. As I remembered I did not wake up from my Fairy world myself. What am I thinking it's not going to work now that I am older? Or will it? I will have to find out later, I wanted to get back to my cabin and Beth, first anyway.

Little Beth was still sleeping, and the Agents were up at the big house now interrogating the Boss man, when I returned. I relieved the agent of his baby-sitting job and he excepted happily to join the others at the house. I am pretty beat but with the curiosity of the necklace waiting to be worn, plus I had to see what would happen when I put it on. Laying quietly on the couch near little Beth, I put it over my head. But nothing happened except I fell into a deep dreamless sleep.

Waking up early in the morning I realize Beth was sitting there waiting for me patently to wake up. "Good morning, Beth. How long have you been up?" I said with a stretch and a yawn.

"Not long. I was so happy to see you back this morning." Her small voice said cheerfully. "I hope you can finish the story this morning, if that would be alright?"

"Umm, sure sweetie but let me get us fed first and I can do that." I got up padded her on the head and took care of the morning necessities. Before breakfast we took Buddy for walk and I was so relieved the Boss man was caught and I could start living my life. Breakfast was muffins and juice. After we ate, we went out on the front porch that was warming in the bright morning sun. We still put on our jackets, with me forgetting mine still had the microphone pin still on it. Now Little Beth started begging me to finish the story. Answering her plea, "Ok I will try to finish the Fairytale of Little Marie."

The Memory

Back at the main house, everyone was settling down with warm coco or coffee and blankets. They were quietly talking, and Little Marie thought this would be her chance to be alone with her necklace. "May I go take a nap Mommy? I will get up before dinner." *She snuggled her Mommy.*

"That is a good idea, maybe all you girls would like to rest before dinner?" *Mommy looked at the other two girls, but they shook their head no, so Mommy hugged Little Marie and told her,* "OK sweetie we will come get you for dinner."

Little Marie didn't wait a moment and ran upstairs, into her room and closed the door. "Oh my, this has been a day. I can't wait to go back and talk to Christina!" *With that still on her mind she put her necklace on. It was an amazing thing every time! She was back but it seemed different. What was it? She looked around finding herself back in the clearing. It was so bright and clear. Everything seemed to sparkle and shine in the light of the day. The sky seemed the brightest blue Little Marie had ever seen. White fluffy clouds made a break for the eye to be able to look into its vastness. Again, everyone was gone. Where should she look? Ah* "Yes, I will go check with Fritz and ask what he knows." *She said out loud.*

As she flew to Shimmering Lake she felt such peace. Knowing the girls were safe in both worlds made her heart jump for joy. "Thank you, Jesus!" *again she said out loud.*

"You are so very welcome my child. I thank you also!" *Jesus smiled as her appeared next to her floating at the same speed she was flying. She slowed in her amazement of His sudden appearance.*

"Oh, it's you. I love you so much Jesus." *Little Marie was so happy she flew into his arms.*

Little Marie Grows Up

He caught her and gently held her while they floated back to the island floor. "I love you more than you know my little one. And look at what we accomplished together." Jesus let her go to show her where they had landed.

It was a beautiful place. The sky was turning all shades of blue, purple and pink behind a small castle on a hill. A waterfall was to the left with the river it made, flowing around the front, under the bridge that led into the entrance of a courtyard.

"This is so very beautiful. I can't believe my eyes. It looks like everyone is there inside the gate, in the court yard. Oh, let's go see." Little Marie said while starting to fly off. But Jesus stayed where He was saying, "In a few moments you will be caught up in all the wonderful excitement of the celebration in the courtyard of Christina's castle. Before that happens, I would like to spend some time alone with you. It is your choice. It might be awhile until such a time just like this."

Little Marie stopped in midair and had to stop only a moment to think. Her love for Jesus was stronger than her excitement of the party below. "Yes, I would like to stay here with you!" He was her first love, now. She flew back to His side and they rested on a rock that just seemed to be there for that purpose. They both took in the lovely seen before them. Little Marie leaned on His arm, and asked "Why might it be awhile until such a time as this?" She spoke softly.

He smiled at her innocence. "There are times in life where so many things like, people, circumstances and the choices people make, become very distracting and they miss the bigger picture or the plan, WE, The Creator, Son and Holy Spirit, are working to our Glory. Our plan is Love, Mercy and Grace for our creation mankind. WE work with the chaos that comes from mankind knowing good and evil, with Man kinds free will and the enemy always trying to tempt them with it. It is always a time to stop and remember, US! We will complete what We started. Our plan will not fail because, it is Finished by what I did on the cross, concurring sin and death. WE now will walk out Our grace, power, and love in each believer in US, because I Am the only way to freedom of all sin and the law that condemns. My blood paid the price for all. It gives freedom to live by grace and not in slaved to the law that brings death, anymore! In me there is no more condemnation. The Holy Spirit lives in my believers. He will work it out in you, by you renewing your mind in Me, which I am also the Word that became flesh, so remain in my word and you well remain in me and your hearts will be changed."

Little Marie ponder these deep revelations, a moment, then replied, "I am not sure, but do You mean I need to remember to take time out with All of you specially when things are going crazy? I can see how that will help me not be so scared or worried when things are out of my control, good or bad!" She then looked into His eyes and was melted to her heart at the love she saw there.

"You are so amazing Little Marie on how you are learning so quickly the lessons you are shown. If you, always remember to continue to grow up in Me, together We will do mighty things in your lifetime." Jesus looked out again to the beautiful scene. They continued to talk for what seemed like hours. As long as Little Marie remained with Him there so did He. She listened and learned and rested in Him.

It was only when she saw the light dimming a bit, she said she would like to go to the party together. As they entered the gate everyone stopped and cheered. "They are here. Hurray to the hero's! Alleluia, praise The Great I AM!" All the creatures and fairies where gathered around Christina and a man with a scar. The air filled with flower petals, sparkles and bubbles. They were all cheering Little Marie now. She was carried away to stand before Christina and the mysterious man. She was so excited and happy.

"Oh, Little Marie we are all so very happy you came into our lives. Things have worked out here in our little Island because you have helped The Great I AM with His plan for Love, Mercy and Grace. Look here my true love Count Christopher has been made new. He was lost to me but now has been found. Thank You for your love and obedience to the Lord we all have been touch by you coming here. Again, we thank Them and you my dear." Christina bowed to her as did all that were present there.

"I didn't do anything. It's was Jesus. You all have helped me, and I am so very glad to know you and this place. I have learned so much and want to know more. Thank you all for your love. Now can I see your beautiful castle Christina?" Little Marie was very humbled by this attention and didn't want all of it for once.

"Yes, of course my dear when there is time. I want you to meet someone special first. Oh Mr. Fritz would you please bring Little Marie to meet *your guest.*" *Christina summoned the fox man and Mr. Fritz ran over to them and whisked Little Marie away into the crowd of well-wishers.*

"*Hello, sweet Marie…*" *Granny said.* "*My, we are so happy to see you.*" *Ginger said. And on it went until they stopped in front of a small beautiful dark-haired lady dressed in ruby satin. She had a small crown adorned with tiny rubies and diamonds.*

"*Oh, how lovely you are Miss?*" *Little Marie could not keep her eyes off the beauty of this young lady.*

"*May I introduce Princess Sarah. And Princess Sarah may I introduce Little Marie our dear friend.*" *Fritz placed Sarah's hand into Little Marie's and bowed.*

Sarah spoke first. "*It is my pleasure and honor to make you acquaintance Miss. Little Marie. I am told you have met my dear sister Crystal. I would love to know about her when you have a moment to talk. I realize that everyone would like to have time with you so I will wait for the appropriate time.*" *Sarah curtsied.*

"*It is my pleasure and much to my surprise to meet you. For you are the very reason I have been on this fantastic adventure, that has forever changed my live. We must spend the time now because I do not know how long I can stay.*" *So Little Marie and Sarah were taken to a quieter place for Little Marie to tell her story. It did not take long and the two returned smiling, arm in arm.*

"*Well that was fast!*" *Mr. Fritz was the first to greet them.*

Sarah ran over to him and grabbed his arm so he would walk with her. "*Why yes Mr. Fritz and what a tale it is!*" *She turned and winked at Little Marie as she walked away into the side rose garden.*

Little Marie waved and then rejoined the party. They were dancing to a very lively tune, so she joined in. As she was dancing taking in all the beauty of the sunset and party, she had realized Jesus was not anywhere to be seen. But before she became worried, she remembered she might not see him, but He was always there! Embracing the peace this brought her, she went back to enjoying herself and the party knowing Jesus was too! Every once and awhile, whispering to Him, "*Thank you, this is so wonderful.*" *As the party was dying down, the fairies and woodland creatures started to make their way home or to the guest rooms provided to those that were staying. Little Marie was surprised she was still here. Mommy hadn't* wakened her up yet. Smiling knowing she had more time she decided to seek out some of her fairy friends still here. Flying up to see what she could do to help she found they seemed preoccupied with all sorts of things. "So sorry my dear, no time to chat. When fairies have a job to do, we do it with focus and determination. No time for anything else until the job is done. Now it seems your time to enjoy and relax is here because you have completed your job, for now." Christina said coming up behind her, then a bit louder she announced, "We are so very thankful to the wonderful Creator for bringing you here. I hope you take all of what you've learned here and keep growing closer to I Am The Father, the Son and the Holy Spirit. Now go and we will see you again!" Christina bent down and kissed Little Marie on the fore head marveling at how Little Marie has grown in wisdom and beauty in such a short time.

Little Marie was moved by her fairy God Mothers kindness and kiss. "Thank you for helping me and showing me, this wondrous world you live. I love you all." Then looking into Christina's beautiful crystal eyes, whispering "I think of all the fairy's, I love you the most." She kissed Christina's hand and flew off to find where her heart was pulling her. At the top of the hills overlooking the castle, she rested looking at the slice of moon now showing above the castles. The stars seemed to twinkle in the sky and she smile pondering all the wonder of the past weeks.

"Oh, what an extra fun night celebrating with everyone, Jesus. I'm so thankful and hope we have more adventures to celebrate." She sat back not expecting a reply for she was alone watching the trees and valleys that sparkled below. But in surprise she was not alone Jesus was sitting beside her once again.

"I am so happy you enjoyed yourself. Little Marie We are with you always and We enjoy you so much. Remember what you have learned and will continue to learn through the lessons in your life in the world. We use them for good even though they are maybe meant for evil by the enemy. The battle is ours but mankind is caught in the middle of it because of free will. The power of choice is not understood by many so mankind makes a lot of powerful mistakes that ripple out to the universe. I finished what needed to be done to cover those mistakes so mankind can walk with Us and together we can heal the land. But without Us it will fall to ruin. Many will choose ruin over the one true Way. But We *know who is Ours, so We are waiting for all to make the choice of life. There is a day coming that We will cleanse and destroy evil on Earth for good, but for now in the battle We work out Our plan of Grace, Love and Mercy though Our People, Our creation."* He looked her in the eyes and finished saying, *"You are so precious to Us. Go into your future with Us and you will experience Our love, power and joy. You have so much more to do in your life. Together you will succeed but apart for Me you can do nothing good because human good can be turned to evil but My good is pure and brings life. It cannot be turned to evil! The lessons of life help humans realize this truth and the choice is theirs alone. To lean on their own understanding or The Creator of them and the universe they live in! His love, power and grace has been shown in Me. You have that power, my beloved Little Marie, as do all who believe and receive my grace and love. Now go out living out that grace with me changing you to be like Us, your makers. Be you Little Marie and enjoy life We are with you!"* He then hugged her and was gone. And someone other than Mommy was waking her up. *"Oh no not yet…"*

"Little Marie wake up we have some great news to tell you!

Knowing You are Loved

The girls where all excited when Misty told them about her talk with "Miss Cindy", her new title. "I really can't believe I might be able to live here, with her away from those people!" Referring to her Mom and step dad.

"Oh, this is so wonderful." Christy commented deep in thought. She was very happy for her friend and even her little sister because Little Marie seemed fine after all that has happened, but what about me! Something still was wrong. No matter how hard she tried she couldn't forget that she was different now. That bad man had changed that. She had bad thoughts now. Her body felt different and she didn't like it. Well here I go again dwelling on that when things were going so well. The kidnappers were caught. Misty won't have to live with her stepdad's abuse, and maybe closer to her because her mommy was marrying Paul and they were sure to live here too! Little Marie seemed to grow up since that day and have some kind of spiritual break through or something. What did he do to her? Maybe it was not the same thing? Weird…because I feel like my life is not mine any more. It has been changed. Something was stolen from me that I don't even understand but I know it was mine and now it's gone. He stole it from me. I hate him and if I could I would kill him! Oh my where did that though come from? Go away I am a good person I am a good person. Before she knew it, she ran out of the room leaving Little Marie and Misty to wonder where. She didn't care she just needed to be by herself and maybe get control of her selfish thoughts. She ran down the stairs and out the front doors without thinking almost running Dr. Strauss over in the process.

"Hello Christy… I was going to ask if I could speak with you for a moment? I could take a walk with you if you don't mind? You seem in a hurry?" Dr. Tiffany called out and followed the surprised young girl.

"UMMM I was going to ah go down by the beach, I guess you could walk with me for a few minutes." Christy had to be nice she had to prove she was still a good girl. She walked purposefully and as fast as her long legs would go.

"I would love to go down to the beach if you don't mind. I have not seen the grounds of this magical place." Dr. Tiffany hoped she used the right term to break through the terrible pain she saw in Christy's eyes.

Christy's good nature came through and she offered to show the Dr. around and little did they know this was the beginning of a healing journey for Christy with Dr. Tiffany. In the end the Dr. will help Christy and her family deal with the after effects of abuse because at any age or time of life, that if not healed, lead to victims to become abusers, if not to others to themselves. Self-shame is by far one of the biggest cause of this continuing cycle. Healing helps to change and stop that cycle. Starting with the heart choosing the truth that each is a wonderful creation all falling short and those that chose to cause pain are in pain themselves Forgiveness is part of the process and is a choice. Then the mind has to then chose to stand focusing on all the positives and growing into a whole person with self-control to fight the mind battles that come from shame and regret. Christy will have many choices and so will the entire family and with hope and a prayer they will find healing, love, mercy and grace!

It will be each in their own ways! Little Marie had dreams and visions. Misty provision through a beautiful blind woman. Mommy- Melissa through a loving generous kind man named Paul. Christy through a wise and caring Doctor named Tiffany. Each was touched and loved by the I Am the Creator, The Son and The Holy Spirit and They work through all for, Their good purpose, for Their beloved children!

All you have to do is look and ask and look to see They are there waiting for you to know Them.

It's up to you and you alone!
Always remember "You are LOVED!"

The end

"What do you think Beth, about my story of Little Marie?" I asked knowing this was the placed I wanted to stop. I wanted to stay there remembering Jesus for a moment.

"It is a wonderful story. I think it happened and I want to know Jesus too." She replied with hope in her voice for the first time.

So, I asked her to pray for exactly that and then we prayed together her confession of faith in the Savior of the world, the I AM- Jesus The Son. Now that's what I call a great ending to a long twenty-four hours. A few minutes later while Beth and I were sitting on the porch in the morning sun, Special Agent James Manchester walked up the path to the steps of the porch.

"Good Morning Ladies, may I join you?" He gestured to the steps and sat down without waiting for an answer. "It is a beautiful morning and is very nice to enjoy it with you lovely ladies."

Beth giggled and leaned into me. "Well we are very pleased to have you." I replied. Then we all sat there enjoying the sounds of the forest for a while longer. Then I broke the silence, "I want to thank you Special Agent James Manchester for all you have done. I am still trying to believe it's all over." I was realizing I might not see him again, so I added, "I am very thankful it was you that was assigned to rescue me, well I mean, all of us!" Oh my God that was way corny? Please let him not think I am dork. Looking away at that thought.

"Well I think at this point I would like you to call me James. It has been my pleasure to be on this assignment and to help solve this case. Mr. Rodney Campbell a.k.a. The Boss man will not be hurting anyone else ever again. The way You, Miss. Marie, handled the pressure of last night, is remarkable. When you forgave the monster that has been against you for so long. Just after confessing to me, what you wanted to do to him, well you know what I mean. By the way that is what broke him, your forgiveness. Before we even started the questioning, he was talking. First, he was angry, but he just kept talking and we kept listening and, in the end, we got a whole lot of information to get closer to the Portland base of the sex traffickers. Then to top it off, I hear the ending to a great story. Marie you're a wonderful story teller. I have been privileged to be able to hear you tell it." He finished by pointing to my jacket with the micro phone pin on it.

With my checks turning red, I had to laugh because I had no idea it was still there. He was making me so comfortable that I forgot he had been listening this whole time. He then reached in his ear and took out the listen device to put in his pocket. I took off the pin and handed it to him. "Ok James, thank you for the encouragement but I must say the story telling is a God thing, if you know what I mean. I have never done it before, but I am sure glad Little Beth, wanted to hear it told." I hugged Beth. Buddy got up from my feet to stretch. I thought to myself, I wish this moment could gone on forever.

"Well, well, that is a beautiful necklace, Marie." James said pointing at me.

"Oh, I forgot my Mom found it and gave it to me last night." I held it out to look at it again.

"Is that Little Marie's necklace? But you are not asleep?" Little Beth asked perplexed.

"I know. I think it worked only for Little Marie, not grown up Marie." I said with a laugh. Thinking maybe I would give it to Beth someday to remember this time.

"Oh ok, it is really pretty." She looked at it one more time then asked, "So, can I take Buddy down to the path for a walk. We won't go far." Beth said in earnest.

I looked at James and he nodded, "That sounds ok to me, we just want to be able to see you."

"Ok but do as the Special Agent says." I agreed with a wink. At that she grabbed Buddies leash and ran down the stairs to walk the dog. The pathway was the view to the water and the forest was thinned out to be my front yard to see through to the cove. "I am so blessed" I thought.

"You are blessed." James said as he got up to come sit, next to me.

"Ha I didn't know I said that out loud. I guess I have been alone so long that I do talk to myself. I read somewhere, it is a healthy thing to do." Why was I rambling? He was sitting right next to me and his knee was touching mine. Oh, wow now he stretched his arm behind my head to rest it on the bench back. I felt giddy like a blushing school girl, again. I just sat there quietly but so nervous. So, I kept watching little Beth and Buddy they had reached the water but stayed on the path playing in the sand. She waved and then played with Buddy. It was so good to see her as a little girl should be at her age.

Then bringing me back to him, he replied, "It is, a good healthy thing as long as it's positive talk in the long run." He smiled wide. Then looking around, he said "You are not alone. You know, this is a very lovely place, Marie. I am blessed right now too." He then turned my head and gave me a powerful kiss, that took my breath away! Looking into his eyes I melted into him and he kissed me again more gently. What was happening. This was so wonderful but crazy. We just met and went through something very intense. Oh, that must be it, we are both transferring our emotions from that experience to having feelings for each other. "Just stop analyzing it Marie!" I heard in my heart. Ok, I don't want to think right now, he is so delicious. So, I kissed him back, contently.

"You are an angel sent from God to me!" He was saying between kisses. Then pulling away he checked on little Beth. He saw her still there with Buddy looking out to sea. "What have you done to me. I am memorized by you, Marie. I want to know everything about you. Yet I feel like I have known you forever. I knew there was something more to you than any other woman I have known. There was always something missing with them, but now." He said then kissed me again.

I had to slow down, this was too overwhelming. I thought I had met my true love and never had the chance to really find out because of the accident. Now I was feeling something more than I had felt for my fiancé. "James, please we need to get some self-control. This is happening to fast. This probably happens after the kind of ordeal we just went through. Don't say things you might regret." I leaned my head on his shoulder not wanting to look into his loving eyes.

He held me and then laughed out loud, "Yes I have heard of that, relations that start after stressful life threating circumstances, do not last. Believe me I know that from my own experience being an FBI Special Agent. I can tell you the truth, this is different, for me anyways. So, you know I understand, and I also know that I did get carried away. Forgive me." He kissed my hand. "I will prove it to you! The is meant to be and we can take it slow. But I will not deny what I feel because it is new and wonderful." With that he lightly kissed my forehead and stood taking my hand to take a walk to where little Beth was sitting on the sand. This was a start to a new adventure in my live and for the first time I can remember, since I was Little Marie, I was completely looking forward to it.

The End

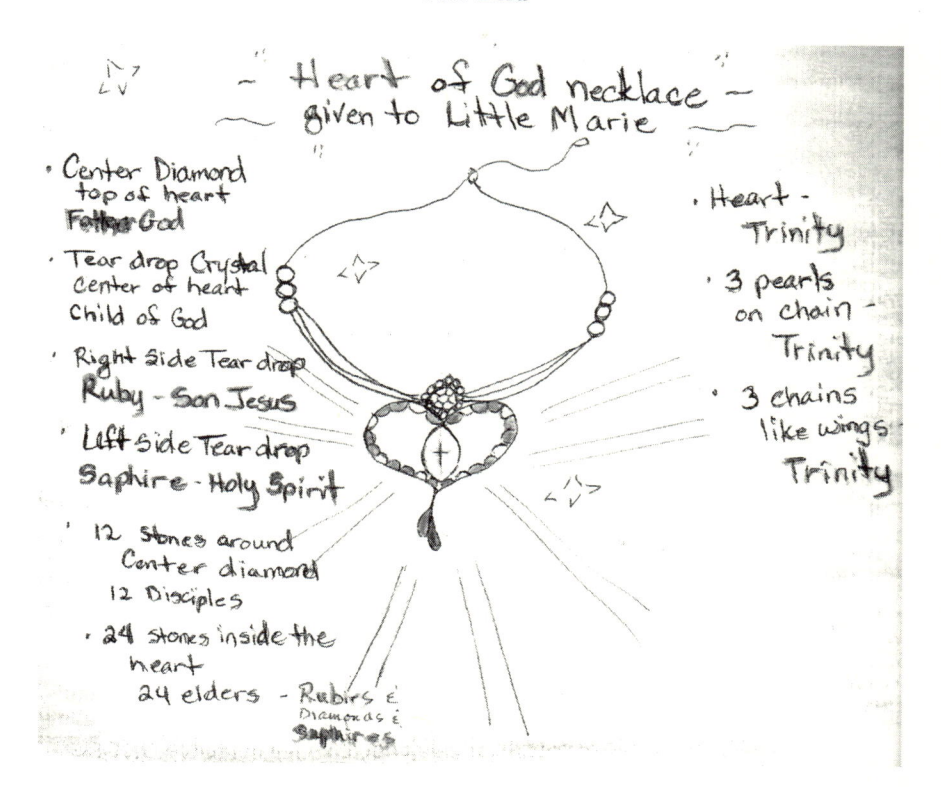

- Heart of God necklace -
given to Little Marie

- Center Diamond
  top of heart
  Father God
- Tear drop Crystal
  center of heart
  Child of God
- Right Side Tear drop
  Ruby - Son Jesus
- Left Side Tear drop
  Saphire - Holy Spirit
- 12 stones around
  Center diamond
  12 Disciples
- 24 stones inside the
  heart
  24 elders - Rubies &
  Diamonds &
  Saphires

- Heart -
  Trinity
- 3 pearls
  on chain -
  Trinity
- 3 chains
  like wings
  Trinity

Prologue: More to Come

I was looking forward to telling James the rest of the story so he understands what happened to my family after the rescue. While lying in his arms after our confession of affection, I asked him, "I'm so glad you like my storytelling because someday I would you like to tell you what happened to some of the characters in my life story that you already have heard in bits and pieces? Special Agent Green was a great help to get Misty, our mayor, to a new place to grow up and recover from her abusive family situation. It will help you understand how Healing Wings became a community and why I'm still a part of it.

"Please I would love to hear it. Only if you tell it like you told the story to little Beth." He said with a laughed.

"I don't know any other way to tell a story. I guess, I will start with Cindy and the Special Agent."

If you or someone you know, is in an abusive situation please reach out for help from one of these resources:

1. *RAINN-1-800-656-(HOPE) 4673*
2. *Local police*
3. *Ministries*
4. *Legal*
5. *Counseling*
6. *Bio-feed Back- reprogramming*

Here are some questions you can ask yourself if you have been abused.

First, of all:

If you are in an abusive situation or relationship right now and need help please call your local police department if possible. Or a family member you trust.

1. Has the Abuser been caught and dealt with? Yes / No

    If No…. Do you need help? Are you Safe? Again, please contact one of the numbers above for help!

2. How long has it been since you told your story to someone? Days_____ Months _____Years _____

    a. Has time helped
    b. Made it worse
    c. Too soon to know yet

3. How did you feel about yourself before the abuse?

4. Now, how do feel and see yourself now?

    a. A Victim
    b. A Survivor
    c. An Overcomer

5. How has the experience changed how you live your life?

6. What are you now thinking about yourself, since becoming free from the abuse and abuser?

7. Have been able to tell someone, you can trust, about your experience's and feeling's?

    a. Has it helped? (You may need someone with training and understanding of being a victim of abuse for positive healing to prevail)

8. How do you handle the PST (Post Traumatic Stress) that comes from memories of the terrible experience that can be triggered at any time?

    a. Does it consume you and cause you to be the victim again?
    b. Can you talk yourself back to the present safety and healing that is occurring every day you chose to overcome the fear and past experiences, by remembering that it's not happening now, telling yourself you are safe and putting the memory away as fast as you can every time with the truth?

**How do you stop thinking about it? "It is only in the mind we have victory! That is where the healing truly begins. What we think and say, we will become. It is our responsibility to control our thoughts. We are the only one that can to do it. As you know, if you don't, others will try to control you and your thoughts with lies and pain. When you are free from that abuser, controller, then it is time to learn the Truth that all civilized human beings were meant to live.

With love, mercy and grace that has been shown from their divine Creator –

    The I Am- The Father, The Son and the Holly Spirit.

Our mind is where the power is and it is also the battlefield for truth and lies, which become beliefs and choses that individual's make. Since mankind has been dealing with trying to control something only the individual has the right to do through proper education, which is mankind's way to become what it was created for –

    Love, mercy and grace.

When that education and common decency are gone then power and pride and lies become what drives those people's lives, which then they try to force others to do their twisted bidding. The abuser against a helpless victim.

To find the truth that sets you free from the creator, is in the Bible and will change your life.
We have the power to choose what we think.
We can choose to be positive or negative even when we may be prone to thinking first one way or the other.

In fact, we are choosing without thinking it, most the time. It is when you start paying attention to your attitude and common sense that you find how many times there is a choice being made.

When we practice thinking through our thoughts and choices with both sides of the brain and the frontal lobe we will become more a where of what truths and lies we are believing which becomes who we are and how we live out our lives.

As healthy growing human beings, productive communities,
Or
Diseased controlled by lies and fear, tearing down the community

Here are some hard questions to ask yourself: (There are no wrong answers)

    9. How do you feel about your abuser?

        a. Fearful
        b. Hatred-Disgust
        c. Revenge
        d. Numb
        e. Confused- Love/Hate
        f. Disconnected
        g. Forgiveness

10. If you were protected and safe, would you want to confront your abuser? Yes No

    If yes what would you say?

11. Do you have hope that healing and a good life are possible?

12. What do you need to be an overcomer?

    a. What have you tried that has helped?
    b. What have you tried that has not helped?

- ❖ Looking back at your answers will help you to see what help you may need from others?
- ❖ It might show you are ready to help others.

Here are resources for you to be an overcomer, not just a victim or survivor!

- ➢ Gods- Word- New Testament
- ➢ Federal and State Agencies
- ➢ Books
- ➢ Support Groups
- ➢ Journaling
- ➢ Education